HOLLY'S GIFT

Small-Town Christmas Wishes Series

JOSIE RIVIERA

PRAISE AND AWARDS

USA TODAY bestselling author

This book is dedicated to all my wonderful readers who have supported me every inch of the way.

THANK YOU!

ABOUT THE SERIES

Welcome to Snowflake, Colorado—a small town where wishes come true! When six old high school friends receive a letter that their fellow friend, Charity Hart, wrote before she passed away, their lives take an unexpected turn. She leaves them each a check for one thousand five hundred dollars and asks them to grant a wish—a secret wish—for someone else by Christmas. And she wants it to be special.

The request sounds simple. After all, they were secret angels in high school together. That's why Charity chose them. But the friends soon discover that it isn't as easy as it seems. With the clock ticking, will they make it happen in time?

Join Mia, Caro, Nate, Taye, Sara, and Holly as they travel down the road to making a wish come true—and take a detour that leads to finding love.

Books in the Series

Mia's Gift (Small-Town Christmas Wishes Series Book 1) by Cindy Flores Martinez

Caro's Gift (Small-Town Christmas Wishes Series Book 2) by Jean C. Gordon

Nate's Gift (Small-Town Christmas Wishes Series Book 3) by Jackie Castle

Sara's Gift (Small-Town Christmas Wishes Series Book 4) by Kimberly Rose Johnson

Holly's Gift (Small-Town Christmas Wishes Series Book 5) by Josie Riviera

Taye's Gift (Small-Town Christmas Wishes Series Book 6) by Pat Simmons

CHAPTER ONE

*H*olly Kim's piano student was always dependable. Well, nearly always. But the wintry weather in Snowflake, Colorado, might have delayed her.

At least, that's what Holly assumed as she peered at her watch for the tenth time in ten minutes.

Rather than remain at her piano bench in her cozy living room, Holly took up a position by the window of her first floor apartment and surveyed the drifting snow covering the tree branches. Dusk edged the gray sky with a pink blush before the sun set, and murky clouds emerged. With less than four weeks remaining until Christmas, the forecast called for freezing temperatures.

And this Thursday was no exception.

She opened the French door separating her living room from the kitchen, then prepared a cup of tea while she waited for Jasmine.

"We prefer a white Christmas season, right, Butterscotch?" Holly expressed her sentiments aloud to the calico cat sitting in a laundry basket in her well-scrubbed kitchen. She'd rescued him from an animal shelter when he was a young adult. He'd been missing half an ear and crawling with fleas, but she'd nursed Butterscotch back to health.

The cat looked up from licking its white paws, but only for an instant. Apparently, paw licking took precedence over Holly's concerns.

As the water in her teapot heated, Holly's thoughts circled back to Jasmine. The child hadn't shown up for her piano lesson the previous week either. And prior to that, Holly had had to cancel two weeks' worth of lessons for all of her students in November, as she had traveled to North Carolina to help take care of her aunt. She'd emailed all her students to notify them. So, for Jasmine, there had been no lesson in a month.

Holly knew that Emily Webster, Jasmine's mother, drove the eleven-year-old girl from their home in Snowflake to Holly's home in Pine Cone Valley every Thursday, then waited outside in her pick-up truck. She also knew that Emily was a single parent.

Despite being unfamiliar with specific aspects of the family situation, Holly had suspected for a number of months that things in the home weren't right. Jasmine and Emily seemed isolated from any other family and friends. And Jasmine, a diligent student who loved playing the piano and had taken lessons for two years, had seemed distracted and listless all Fall.

"Is anything wrong?" Holly had asked Jasmine in late September. As a professional teacher, she chose not to pry into a personal situation, even though she'd developed a genuine bond with the girl.

"Nope," came Jasmine's typical close-mouthed reply. "Everything's fine."

Yet, when it came time to pay her October tuition, Jasmine declared that she'd forgotten the check.

"Tell your mother not to worry about payment," Holly

said. "I'm happy to teach you at no charge. You're a promising student, and I expect you'll become a fine pianist."

On the few instances when Holly had spoken with Emily, a withdrawn woman wearing shapeless clothes, she'd seemed rushed and hadn't met Holly's gaze. Jasmine was an only child, she'd explained.

After pouring boiling water into a ceramic mug, Holly lifted the window blinds and peered out onto her small garden. More snow, collecting quicker now.

Earlier that day, she'd baked Chinese Christmas cookies which had cooled on wire trays on her granite countertop all afternoon.

She plated a cookie, placed an herbal tea bag into her mug to brew, then flicked a glance at her watch again.

With a sigh, she stepped into the living room. She placed her mug on a garden stool she used as a side table, nibbled at the cookie, then sat at her spinet piano. A Chopin nocturne she'd memorized in college flowed easily, and her fingertips glided over the keys. The music was hauntingly beautiful, and Holly paused after the opening measures.

Each time she played a chord, she thought of Jasmine. When she finished, she gathered up the holiday sheet music she'd intended to teach her, which included a duet arrangement of "Silent Night." Unexpectedly, tears gathered in her eyes.

The living room was quiet. Too quiet. The clock on the mantel heralded the seconds with a near-silent tick.

Quiet. Something she'd avoided for weeks. Times like this.

Time to think.

About life. About sorrow. About the death of a friend.

Because of her sad thoughts, Holly picked up her cell phone and rang her aunt Clementine in North Carolina to bolster her spirits.

In her sixties, plump and with age spots on her fragile skin, Holly surmised that Aunt Clementine would be either at her preferred vantage point—sitting on the front porch swing watching the neighbors' activities—or caring for her rescue dogs.

Her aunt answered immediately. "Holly, I recognized your caller ID. Hang on a second—" Her warmhearted voice was invariably a comfort to Holly, as was the recognizable barking of Angel, one of the current rescues, a pint-sized, skinny cocker spaniel with intelligent eyes and soft brown fur.

"Has Angel gained any weight since I left?" Holly asked.

"All she does is eat, and the vet told me that her health has done a complete about-face."

Holly recalled with crystal clarity the two weeks she'd spent with her aunt in November while Clementine had convalesced from hip surgery, and Angel's face-to-face doggy kisses and demands for belly rubs.

As if on cue, a dog barked.

"Is this a good time to talk?" Holly asked. "I'm waiting for a student and hoping she'll still show up."

Holly visualized her aunt wrapping a crocheted shawl around her shoulders, then busying herself with filling Angel's water bowl. "Anything in particular you'd like to discuss?"

"The loss of my wonderful friend."

"Charity Hart." Her aunt paused. "I'm sorry you weren't able to attend her funeral because you stayed to help me."

"I wanted you to get back on your feet." Holly said.

Aunt Clementine was a caring, giving person, much like Charity. However, unlike Charity, who'd longed for a husband and children, Aunt Clementine was a confirmed spinster.

"Besides, I love spending time in the Carolinas." Holly injected a note of levity into an otherwise somber conversation and subsequently failed when her voice caught. In the preceding days, she'd sought to suppress the high school memories, and now they were flashing before her eyes.

"I can't believe she's gone," Holly said. "Charity never uttered a bad word about anyone. When we first met, I was a little skittish after hearing about her reputation."

"Good or bad?"

"The best." Holly took another bite of her cookie, relishing the crunch of chow mein noodles and peanuts. "She cultivated relationships with everybody and wasn't focused on other people's opinions. Her giving came from her sweet heart. She did the right thing, all day, every day."

"Did she always live in Snowflake?"

"She left to attend college in Denver." Holly cradled the phone on her shoulder as she drank her tea. "But after her diagnosis, she chose to live with her mother."

And then, two weeks before Thanksgiving, Charity died.

"Don't cry for me," she'd told her mother, told her friends. "God is faithful."

"You mentioned she left no husband or children?" Aunt Clementine asked.

"She said she'd know when God placed the right man in her life."

Unlike herself, Holly thought, since she'd done the marriage part and failed miserably. Jim, her ex, was cruel and interested only in himself. He'd committed infidelity, left her and initiated the divorce. She'd been broken, fighting a loneliness so deep that she'd turned inward while she desperately tried to maintain an outward composure.

Marrying him had proved that she wasn't cut out for dating and men and happily-ever-after.

Awash with uncomfortable remembrances, she swept Jim from her mind and focused on the loss of her friend.

"Charity was a servant of God," her aunt said.

Holly nodded into the phone. "We attended Bible club

together and studied scripture at our youth group. We'd sit in the front row and take notes."

"I imagine you heeded the pastor's words in respectful silence."

"Well, with a little giggling now and then," she admitted.

They were young then. Now, in their early thirties, they were still young.

"Is Pastor Tom still the pastor at Snowflake Chapel?"

"He is," Holly said, "along with the associate pastor, Manuel Cruz, and his wife, Alma. Whenever I'm the substitute pianist, I see them." Otherwise, she attended her local church in Pine Cone Valley.

At the same moment that she spoke, Holly stood and wandered to the enormous picture window overlooking the street. Outside, the ground shimmered a glistening, icy silver.

It had been a late afternoon much like this one when she'd first met Charity. In turn, Charity had introduced Holly to her friends—Caro, Taye, Sara, Nate, and Mia. They all became instant comrades for they shared a common denominator: They were all Christians. Over the years, they'd remained friends, though some had moved away.

"Holly, are you still there?" her aunt asked.

"Sorry, Aunt Clementine. I was thinking. You may not remember, but during Christmas winter break of my senior year, several of us decided to gift a special person with something we had chosen."

"And who was your special person?"

"It was a secret, which made the activity more delightful and memorable."

"Who did you choose, dear?" her aunt repeated.

"I chose you." Holly smiled, assuming she could divulge her secret after all these years. "You lived in Snowflake at the time, not far from my parents."

Her aunt chuckled.

"I bought you a picture album and filled it with photos of our family," Holly continued, "so you could recall our fun times."

Secret Angels, Charity had declared.

"I wondered who delivered that photo album wrapped in red polka-dot paper and tied with twine. The doorbell rang, but when I opened the door, no one stood there."

Holly giggled. "And now you know."

"I suspected, but was never certain. That album was filled with many precious images, and your mother and I were as close as two sisters could be."

Holly fingered the sterling silver charm bracelet she always wore, a beloved memory of her mother's thoughtfulness. Each charm signified important events in Holly's life—a piano, a flag of South Korea, and her graduation.

"Equally important was the gift of your time and interest," her aunt went on. "I can't tell you how much I appreciate your kindness."

"Nothing's changed. You were like a mother to me after my parents died."

Holly experienced another rush of sadness for another loss. Her adoptive parents had died while serving as missionaries overseas, and it wasn't supposed to happen that way. They were compassionate citizens, trying to help others.

As usual, her aunt was spot on. Time with loved ones was the most precious gift.

Time.

She should have made time to visit Charity when she got sick, Holly thought. But by the time she'd come home to Colorado, Charity had passed.

Truly, it was better to give than to receive. And Charity had offered Holly a precious gift—the gift of an irreplaceable friendship.

Walk with the wise and become wise, for a companion of fools suffers harm. Holly's favorite Scripture verse, Proverbs 13:20, came to mind. Such accurate words—the guardrails that kept her on a straight path that she largely attributed to Charity.

"I didn't keep in touch with her as much as I should have, Aunt Clementine."

"Life gets in the way sometimes. But you mentioned that Charity had moved to Denver."

"Still, we lived in the same state. We relied on social media to stay connected." Holly readied for the pep talk she assumed her aunt was about to offer.

"I understand all about young people and social media," came her aunt's response. "Everyone is connected nowadays."

Though in reality, were they? What was better than a face-to-face chat with an extraordinary friend or loved one?

"We're all busy," Charity had assured Holly when they'd video chatted one chilly evening. "The main thing is we are serving the Lord. God granted us his mercy and forgives our sins every single day. So praise him every single day."

Every single day.

But that's where the similarity ended. Yes, they were both Christians, but unlike Holly, Charity had lived up to her name and continued her charitable giving. Whereas, Holly had not.

"Thanks for chatting with me, Aunt Clementine." Holly peered at the wooden clock perched on the fireplace mantel. "I'm going to call my student. I tried last week when Jasmine missed her lesson, but wasn't able to reach her and left a message. She's my last lesson for tonight."

"Good luck. I love you, dear," Aunt Clementine said.

"I love you too. I'll phone again soon."

Holly clicked off and walked over to her desk by the piano. The certified letter from Green and Sons Law Firm lay open, the first page exactly where she had left it.

In Charity's handwriting, she'd added a note along with the letter:

"Dear Holly, please use this $1500 check to give someone special a wonderful Christmas. Remember all those fun times in high school? Create that magic again. For me."

Consequently, Holly had phoned Don, the lawyer at the firm, who confirmed that each of their friends had received the same amount of money.

In their conversation, Don reminded Holly that if she didn't wish to disperse her check, she had the option to refuse and the firm would donate the money to a worthy cause.

So far, Holly had done nothing except for that quick call to the lawyer's office saying she'd received the check while staying in North Carolina with her aunt. Since returning, she'd let the check sit on her desk and neglected it, as if acknowledging the letter would make her friend's death absolute.

Should she keep it? Because she certainly had no charitable cause in mind.

Another glance at her watch confirmed that Jasmine was now thirty minutes late.

The girl wasn't just late. She wasn't going to show up.

With a worried frown, Holly scrolled through her student contacts and tapped in the number Jasmine had given her when the girl first enrolled for lessons.

"This number is not in service," came the recorded message. "Please check the number and dial again."

Odd, because the number had been in service the previous week.

Holly took a deep pained breath. She should have known something was wrong. *She should have known.*

She doubled through her contacts until she found Jasmine's address.

"I'll drive into Snowflake," she announced to Butterscotch

as she headed for the kitchen. She gulped a last mouthful of tea and set her mug in the stainless steel sink.

In the foyer, she surveyed herself in the mirror and tamed her straight black hair into a semblance of a style. She'd worn navy slacks, a white chenille sweater, and brown leather loafers for teaching. Now she switched her loafers for knee-high boots and drew on a crimson-red wool coat, a knitted green beanie, and gloves.

Her stomach churned as worst-case scenarios raced through her mind. Suppose something had happened to Jasmine and her mother?

Holly expelled a breath, grabbed her car keys and rushed out the door into a bitter cold evening.

CHAPTER TWO

*U*nder fifty minutes later, Holly reached Snowflake. As always, her windshield wipers carved out a clear spot for her to peep through, and she handled her four-wheel-drive Jeep with proficiency. Fortunately, the weather had calmed by the time she arrived, and only a thin layer of slush coated the roads and walkways. She'd adhered to the speed limits, although she preferred to drive fast, with the adventurous assertiveness and bold disregard of peril that was uniquely part of her parents' legacy. Similarly, they'd loved watching NASCAR on television.

However, she reserved her stock-car racing passion for when she visited Aunt Clementine in North Carolina, and attended live events.

She typed Jasmine's address into her phone's GPS and soon discovered there was no such address.

Fake phone number. Fake street address.

Holly envisioned Jasmine's round angelic face, her blond curls arranged into two pigtails. Whenever Holly complimented her piano playing, the girl would blush to the roots of her hair.

Well, the numbers might be fake, but the wonderfully artistic child was real.

So, where was she?

Holly clutched the neckline of her coat and took a deep breath to calm herself.

"Snowflake Homeless Shelter," she said aloud. She'd volunteered at the shelter with friends from church and knew it was located near Blue Spruce Plaza. It had been set up for single mothers and families who needed emergency, temporary shelter.

She brushed the snow off her Jeep with the foam brush she kept in the glove compartment, then hopped back inside. As she drove closer to the town center, she admired the stores festively adorned for Christmas. Lampposts on Main Street were graced with red satin bows and wreaths, and white lights twinkled from boutiques and mom-and-pop shops.

She hung a left and pulled to the curb of the homeless shelter a few minutes later.

Her boots clicked on the shoveled concrete sidewalk as she walked to the entrance. A pavilion was piled with plastic garbage bags crammed with personal possessions and damaged, street-worn luggage. She opted for the wheelchair ramp and shook snow from her coat sleeves.

When she entered the shelter, turmoil greeted her. The smell of cheap industrial cleaner made her hang back. Women, many holding young children, were grouped near an enclosure where an employee worked. A woman in a wheelchair waited silently in the hallway, and a handful of orange tabby kittens looped through the crowd.

At the far end of the lobby rose an undecorated five-foot Scotch pine.

Two men, a slightly hunched, heavyset man with gray hair and a tall good-looking man she guessed to be in his thirties, hardly spared her a second look. Nonetheless, they seemed the most official, so she waited for them to acknowledge her.

"Stand in line over there, miss," the heavyset man said to her. "You'll get a ticket for some clothing and a bed, and a list of shelter rules."

Holly shook her head. "Sir, I'm not here for—"

"Apologies if you're hungry," he said with a harried glance. "Ask a staff member to unlock the refrigerator. We have bottled water, tuna, or peanut butter and jelly sandwiches."

"I've eaten dinner, thanks," Holly replied. "I'm looking for someone."

"You'll be able to find that someone real soon." He glared at the younger man, his blue eyes sparking. "All the residents have been asked to leave."

"Why?" She stepped back. "It's freezing cold out there."

"I've lived here all my life, miss, and am conscious about a Colorado winter and the danger it presents. Nonetheless, tell that to Tim, our hotshot inspector. He thinks we're in the middle of July." Lou stroked his thick white mustache and scowled.

"Lou, I'm not the bad guy here." Tim seemed to hold his irritation in check with an apologetic exhale. Absentmindedly, he pushed a lock of wavy-brown hair off his forehead and granted Holly a slight smile.

She didn't expect to be attracted to a man in a place like this, with its utter chaos and people swarming everywhere.

But she was.

A glimmer of concern in his deep brown eyes gave her pause. Self-consciously, she worried her knitted beanie with her gloved hands. She'd yanked it off when she'd entered the building and consequently assumed her hair was a staticky mess, the ends sticking straight out in all directions. Adding to her disheveled appearance, she knew any lip gloss she'd applied that morning had faded.

And still, he regarded her with interest.

"Hello," he said.

"Hi." She looped the straps of her purse over her shoulder and offered a faint smile.

Normally, she was unimpressed by extraordinarily handsome men. In her experience, they were oftentimes hollow and superficial, or, like her ex-husband, self-absorbed. But this man threw her totally off balance, because his voice sounded soothing in the disorder that surrounded them.

He towered over her, his muscular shoulders impeding everything but her view of him.

And for some reason, he looked vaguely familiar.

"I told you, Tim," Lou was saying. "All the permits, including the electricity, should be in order."

Tim shook his head. "I'm forced to execute city regulations. You realize that. If this problem isn't taken care of it could lead to a fire hazard."

"I can't turn all these homeless people away. Where are they supposed to go?" Lou pivoted and pointed to the Scotch pine in the corner. "What about the tree-trimming party? The children are looking forward to decorating for Christmas."

"Fortunately, you have the weekend. While everyone is decorating, begin making arrangements at the hotels here in town," Tim responded. "There's the Blue Jay Motel and Rocky Mountain Bed and Breakfast."

"For thirty single women and their children?" Lou asked harshly. "The bed and breakfast has six rooms."

"I know the owner, Theresa Rose."

"So do I, and she's usually fully booked," Lou countered. "I suppose you expect the motel to accommodate everyone?"

"Of course not." Tim tapped a forefinger on his lower lip. "How about the Snowflake Inn?"

Lou cast a long-suffering scowl. "All eight suites?"

"There's the Blue Spruce Apartments."

"You mean the Blue Spruce *rented* apartments?"

Tim reacted as if he'd been punched in the stomach. He leaned over and made a pleading gesture with his hands.

"I'm sorry," he said to Lou, although his expression was set.

"Make way," an EMT shouted, steering a gurney into the hallway.

Holly hustled to the side to let them through.

"What's going on?" she asked the woman in the wheelchair. Her boots were hardly worn, and Holly surmised they'd been donated.

"Lou had to call for an ambulance a little bit ago. Old lady Alley fell off her bunk bed again." The woman put a fistful of coins into the vending machine and tugged out a bag of chips. She grinned, displaying a row of missing teeth. "She's a longer term resident and claimed the top bunk in a semiprivate room. Last time this happened, she split her head on the concrete floor." She wheeled to the window and gawked at the ambulance stationed at the curb, its blinking lights steadily flashing through the shelter's windows.

Holly trained her attention back to the two men.

"Who will pay for all these rooms?" Lou pointed a gnarled finger at Tim.

"Look, I don't want to quarrel. If there was something I could do, I would do it," Tim shot back. "But as it stands now, the shelter needs to close."

"Impossible."

"It won't be forever, just until we get this problem sorted. That's the best I can do."

"Then your best isn't good enough."

"I wish I could offer more," Tim replied in a chillingly polite manner. "But I can't."

CHAPTER THREE

imothy Stewart watched Lou stalk down the hallway. Again and again, he'd deflected Lou's questions because he didn't have an answer. He'd expected to sway Lou's animosity by explaining the residents' safety and the city of Snowflake's concerns.

It had been to no avail.

"I'm phoning Mayor Hardy," Lou muttered over his shoulder, half to himself.

"I said I was sorry twice now," Tim replied loudly, but not loudly enough, since Lou didn't swing around.

For the second time, Tim regarded the beautiful Asian woman standing near the vending machine. Too stressed to do anything else, he shoved his hands into his jean pockets. "I'm truly sorry about this," he said to no one in particular.

Apparently overhearing him, she nodded. "Now that's another apology."

He pushed his hair back with a shaking hand. "Do you need something, miss ...?" He heard the impatience in his tone, which he blamed on fatigue and the pressure of a wearying day.

"No, I assume *you're* certainly not the one who can help."
Great. Just great. More blame.

Lou's words continued to hammer into Tim's brain. Even his best wasn't good enough.

He stretched a wool cap over his ears, conscious that the woman was staring at him. Her dark almond-shaped eyes were magnificent, her cheekbones prominent.

And she was extremely attractive.

He shook his head. She was certainly a complication he didn't need.

In order to avoid her stare, his gaze flitted to the window. The ambulance threw on the siren and sped away.

People were hurt all the time, physically and emotionally. Which hurt worst?

With no other place to look, he met her stare. "Lou is a friend," he explained.

Why he suddenly felt that he should clarify anything to anyone, especially a stranger, was beyond him.

"Right. I can see you are best buddies." Ruefully, she shook her head. Her mouth held the hint of a smile.

Debating whether to grin or scowl, he summed up his indecision by offering a rueful shrug.

He was supposed to have clocked out of work two hours ago, yet he'd stayed, unsuccessfully trying to fix the shelter's electric problem. He was an inspector, not an electrician, he'd finally reminded himself when, frustrated, he'd given up.

And now, as a result for his concern, he was being chastised by an attractive homeless woman.

"Were you waiting for a bed, miss?" Tim gestured to the line by the glass enclosure, all impatient to be checked in. Viewing the foyer, he noted a woman in a wheelchair munching on a bag of chips.

Holiday stockings were piled high on a table against a wall, along with a miniature Christmas card village. A kitten wound around his legs, and he picked it up to stroke the velvety fur.

"Your friend already asked me." The attractive woman said, as her gaze met his. "I don't need a bed or a meal. I'm searching for a mother and her daughter."

For a lengthy moment, Tim truly assessed her, and consequently, two things hit him at once.

First, she had a wonderful smile, and second, her soft, gorgeous eyes were brimming with … bemusement.

Since gazing at her was infinitely better than worrying about the homeless shelter and a decision he couldn't control, he preferred to gaze at her. There was a vivaciousness about her, the way her silky straight black hair hung loose around her face. And her profile, the pert, turned-up nose, her shoulders rigidly set, were all adorable.

He doubted she'd appreciate his observations.

"May I ask your age?" he inquired, then cringed at his audacity for asking such a question.

She flashed a smile. "I'm almost thirty-three. Why?"

"You don't look a day over twenty-one."

"My birthday is January first." She flavored her response with levity. "So, I'll look older in a month."

He grinned. "A New Year's baby?"

"I am, yes."

She didn't appear to be the average shelter resident, but because of his past, he knew well how appearances were deceiving. His mother hadn't looked like she lived in a homeless shelter, either. And she'd made certain that she and Tim were always clean and tidy.

"Who might have information concerning this woman and her daughter?" the woman asked.

"Speak to Lou." Tim shifted. "He pretty much runs things around here."

"Lou is facing bigger problems these days." She gazed out

the window where a few women stood and Tim followed her gaze. To fight off the cold, the women shivered and clutched thin coats to their shoulders.

"Right." With an exasperated sigh, Tim set down the kitten. "Bigger problems."

"Finding rooms for all these people in one weekend is a big undertaking."

"I'm well aware of the situation." As a result of him creating it, although he'd only been following orders. "What I meant was, why are you looking for this mother and daughter?"

"Because I want to help them."

"Is this a good Christmas deed or something?" he asked. "The shelter is already supported by generous private donations."

"Hmm. If you look around, we can both agree the donations apparently aren't generous enough."

"The contributions are reliable and support the day-to-day expenses." He ignored her killing frown. Apparently his explanation wasn't helping the situation. "Though rewiring a place this old will cost thousands of dollars."

"How about prayer?" she asked.

"How about it?"

"Prayer will help."

He lifted an eyebrow. "How about money? Money will really help."

"You sound like a cynic. Some call it an escape so that they don't get wounded."

"So now you're analyzing me?"

"Hardly. I'm just stating a fact." She surveyed the people waiting. "All I'm suggesting is to have faith too."

Faith. God. When was the last time anyone had mentioned either to him? Probably his grandmother when he was a child. But it was more comfortable believing in nothing, and that was the way he intended to keep things.

Consequently, he was never hurt. He'd learned early on that if he relied only on himself, at least he could depend on someone.

She was evidently waiting for a reply, so he extended his right hand. "I'm Tim."

"I gathered."

"Tim Stewart." His hand was still outstretched, yet she wavered. He pressed his lips together. "And you are?"

"Holly. Holly Kim."

"You're Asian?"

She smiled. "Yes."

"Chinese?"

"Korean. We have a rounder face."

The way she watched him, with gentleness in her strikingly expressive eyes, caused him to stand still. His mother had never looked at him with such consideration. Similarly, neither had his girlfriend of the past six months.

"You live here in Snowflake?" he inquired.

A blink of a hesitation before Holly responded. "I live in Pine Cone Valley."

"About an hour away, right?"

"Under an hour, depending on how fast you drive."

"I can't imagine someone like you would ever buck the speed limit." He shot her a look of amusement. "You don't seem the type."

"And what type is that, Tim?"

A biased stereotype. He expected a blue-eyed blond wearing a tight skirt to drive fast cars, not a demure Asian woman. Noting Holly's scowl, he wisely didn't express his sentiments aloud.

"I meant—I'm a type." He congratulated himself for shifting the topic so effortlessly.

"Oh, really. What type is that?"

"I suppose I *am* a cynic when it comes to faith and religion." He offered a contrite head shake, then zipped up his navy-blue quilted parka. "But for the record, I don't have the patience for God."

"Did God take too long to answer your prayers?"

"I don't know. He's never answered any."

"Perhaps faith will produce patience so that you can trust again."

"For instance, you mean trust in God?" he countered. "Or trust in others?"

"Both."

"Right." His shrug meant just the opposite. *Wrong.*

He had sent endless prayers to heaven throughout his adolescence, asking God to change his family's situation. Instead, Tim and his mother had slept beneath bridges when the shelters in Denver were full. Free weekly newspapers served as their blankets.

Of course that was when they weren't joy riding on country roads with her so-called buddies who were forever intent on partying. If the scene involved booze, his mother was the first to arrive, oftentimes with Tim in tow.

"I understand," Holly said.

His gaze narrowed on her smile. He had the edgy feeling that she was one of those people who might try to convert him to her way of thinking. An evangelist—someone who fancied Gospel preaching and spreading the Good Word.

"Well? Is there a way I can locate them?" Behind her beautiful face was a determination that caught him off guard.

"All the women and children are housed down the hall," he said even as his radar went up. Once, his mother had mistakenly depended on individuals who claimed they wanted to help her and her son. "Call the shelter later. Or, if you wait, things should quiet in an hour."

Her shoulders stiffened. He hadn't meant to sound curt, but the day had been long and disheartening.

"Call who?" she asked.

"The shelter, miss—"

"Holly," she reminded him.

"Holly, I'm one of two building inspectors in Snowflake. I don't work here. Their exact hours are posted somewhere."

"I assume they welcome visitors day and night." She rubbed the middle of her forehead. "So the shelter really must close?"

"Yes." He steered them to an out of the way corner. "I don't make the rules, I just enforce them."

"No need to get defensive, Mr. ..."

Had he been defensive? He exhaled. *Yeah, probably.*

"Tim. Tim Stewart," he said. Was he really that forget-table? Who else walked away from a promising acting career?

Someone who was disillusioned.

He'd certainly felt that way when he was young—invisible in a sea of high school students as he and his mother moved from place to place. Ten schools in as many years, and being the new kid wasn't fun, especially as he entered adolescence.

"What happened?" Holly asked. "Why wasn't anyone aware of this electrical problem sooner?"

He was surprised her tone wasn't incriminating, especially since he'd been so abrupt with her. His gaze lingered on her lovely features. Her complexion was slightly golden, her high cheekbones flushed. Her lips were full, a deep vivid pink.

Slight and slim, she couldn't weigh more than a hundred pounds soaking wet.

And as he continued staring, he was utterly, inexplicably drawn to her.

In the silence, she waited for an explanation.

His hands dropped to his sides. "The electricity isn't up to code," he replied.

She nodded. "Go on."

His phone pinged, indicating an incoming text. He withdrew it from his pocket, assuming it was Felicia, his on-again, off-again girlfriend. He glanced at the screen. Sure enough, she was asking why he hadn't picked her up for dinner yet.

Soon. Tied up at work, he rapidly texted, then jammed the phone back in his pocket.

"Sorry," he said to Holly. "You were asking?"

"About the electricity for the building."

"The shelter lost power twice this week, and the ancient wiring presents a safety hazard."

She peered around. "Then all the more reason for me to find the family."

Lou stomped over. "You still here, Mr. Hot Shot Movie Star Inspector?"

"I was just leaving," Tim replied.

"Movie star?" Holly looked up at him. "I thought I recognized you."

"It was many years ago, and it was actually a television series." Tim dismissed her question by gesturing to Lou. "As I said, here's the guy to talk to if he can spare a minute."

Holly turned to Lou. "I'm Holly Kim. I'm aware this is a bad time, but I'm looking for—"

"Miss Kim, I'm so sorry I haven't been to my piano lessons." A girl about eleven years old raced to Holly and threw her skinny arms around Holly's waist. Her huge green eyes reminded Tim of a street urchin. "My mother lost your phone number."

"Jasmine, I'm so relieved you are here." Holly crouched down and cupped the little girl's face in her hands. "I was beyond worried. I called the number your mother had given me, then went to your address and—"

A woman with pinched cheeks and sunken gray eyes, her mousey-brown hair scraped back by a tortoise-colored plastic clasp, hurried down the hall. She gripped a self-improvement book close to her chest. She looked anxious, as if she never was able to catch up with life and couldn't quite handle it.

Tim recognized the look, for he'd seen it often enough on his mother's face. This woman had an addiction, most likely alcohol.

"Miss Kim, I apologize." The woman advanced toward Holly. "My truck wouldn't start tonight."

"I'm just glad you're okay, Emily," Miss Kim replied.

"Mommy." Jasmine tugged at her mother's sleeve. "We don't have a truck anymore. Remember at Sunday morning service the pastor told us not to lie?"

"Yes, yes." Emily's voice was quick and impatient. "I'm not perfect, you know."

Tim dawdled by the doorway, pretending to check his phone as he readied to leave. Yes, he was eavesdropping, but he couldn't help himself.

Thus, Miss Holly Kim was a piano teacher, and she obviously had an indisputable attachment to the young girl. And she didn't live in Snowflake.

He was familiar with Pine Cone Valley, recalling that the town boasted an excellent coffee shop rivaling the Cozy Coffee Shop in Snowflake. Maybe he could invite her for coffee and a sandwich sometime.

And why would he do that? Inwardly, he reined in his thoughts.

Complications, complications.

"Tim," Lou called. "Is there any other way?"

"I wish there were, Lou." He blew out a frustrated breath. "To sum everything up, I'll be back first thing Monday to close the place."

He glanced toward the entrance. At least the good-natured giggling between two teenage residents, both wearing similar flannel shirts and torn jeans, took his mind off the problem for a moment.

"Thanks for nothing," Lou muttered, stamping away again.

So now what?

Tim lingered by the doorway. Should he say good-bye to Holly, mumble a "nice to have met you," or just leave the building?

He'd been curt with her but he'd apologized, hadn't he?

Umm, no, in fact, he hadn't. And the tension he'd felt all evening had spun an attraction to her he couldn't explain.

Really, tension could do that?

In his case, yes. Or rather, the real reason. He simply wanted to see her again.

He hung back, but merely for a second before he strode to her. She was conversing with Jasmine's mother, while Jasmine munched on a handful of chips the woman in the wheelchair shared with her.

"Holly?" He tapped her on the shoulder.

She excused herself from the conversation and curved to him. "Yes?"

"Can I call you?"

She blinked. "What?"

"Call you. You know, so that we can go out on a date."

"A date? Why?"

"I thought maybe we could go for coffee or something." He was talking like an idiot. Again, he reminded himself he'd had a very long day.

"Why?" she repeated.

"You do drink coffee, don't you?"

"Every morning. But only in the mornings."

"Are you dating anyone?"

"No. Not that it's any of your business." She combed a hand through her hair. "Are you?"

"Am I what?"

"Dating anyone?"

His conscience chattered for no reason, because he and Felicia had an understanding. No long-term commitments.

"I'm not the Grinch who stole Christmas," he said, "if that's what's holding you back."

"You're not grouchy?"

"Hardly ever."

She seemed to be holding in a smile. "So you don't live in a cave?"

"I've never stolen a Christmas, or any other item in my life."

Even at their lowest point, when he and his mother were desperate for a hot meal, at least they hadn't lifted any items out of the convenience stores they'd slipped in to escape a freezing winter's night.

"Thanks, but I'm not interested." Holly's reply was quick, dousing his enthusiasm.

"Why not?"

"I don't date."

A gorgeous woman like her?

Despite the facts that their paths might not cross again and her life was in the next town over, he was interested in getting to know her better. Nonetheless, after the crushing reality of being raised by a neglectful mother, he only dated women who didn't demand more than he could give.

Then again, Holly didn't seem like that kind of woman.

"I can call you," he heard himself saying. "Or text, if you give me your number."

"No call, no coffee, no texts. Understand?"

All right then. This was a set-down he couldn't refute.

He hid his disappointment behind a brief grin. "I understand, loud and clear." He should say more, something sharp and witty, something flippant, but words eluded him. Because in truth, he felt hurt and disheartened.

"Well, good night." He acknowledged the girl's mother and then noticed how Jasmine eyed the vending machine longingly.

He made his way to her. "Hold out your hand," he instructed.

She lifted her freckled face and chortled as he placed a fistful of loose change in her hand.

"Enjoy." He tousled her blond bangs that hung over her eyes. "Buy whatever you want.

She cast a furtive peep at her mother. "Can I get candy?"

"Yes," Emily replied, "since we've eaten supper already. Though don't eat it all at once."

"Yay! I love caramels!" As the change clinked into the machine, Jasmine whirled to give Tim a high-five. "Thanks, Mr. ..."

"Stewart. Tim Stewart."

The woman in the wheelchair backed up, and he automatically gave her a hand, straightening her toward the hallway that led to the residents' rooms. Behind him, he overheard his name whispered, and not in a flattering way. Puzzled, worried glances were cast at him. Apparently word traveled fast, because he was already slated as the guy who was shutting down the place right before Christmas.

With an offhand nod, he turned toward the door and almost collided with a resident shuffling across the lobby.

He spun to find Holly watching him. He bid her and her friends a cordial good night and added a brief smile.

She smiled back, but the smile didn't reach her eyes.

She didn't want him to call her, since she didn't want to date him, or anyone by the sounds of it. She didn't like coffee in the afternoon, or phone calls, or texts.

So that was settled.

He'd never had to pursue a woman before and he wouldn't start now, especially with one who wasn't interested.

He tugged on his wool tweed cap and wound a cranberry-colored scarf around his neck. Many had called him a fool when he'd headed for California as soon as he'd graduated from high school.

Sure, it was a year later than everyone else, but that he blamed on his constant moves. The main thing was, despite the years in between, he'd persevered.

And then, the poor kid from nowhere had landed an acting role.

Therefore, when had adversity ever stopped him?

"I hope to see you again, Holly," he called out.

She opened her mouth to reply, but he strode out the entrance, past the women smoking, the young twenty-some-things making their way inside, the piles of plastic bags jammed with folks' lives. He nodded at the police officer patrolling the area and kept walking.

Again, his cell phone pinged with an incoming text.

This time he ignored it.

CHAPTER FOUR

*A*fter she returned to her apartment later that evening, Holly set Charity's letter on the garden stool in the living room.

With a mug of steaming chamomile tea and a slice of toast slathered with butter, she settled on her tufted couch with Butterscotch curled at her side.

When her landlord had granted permission, she'd wallpapered the room in faux, natural-looking grass cloth that sported a knotted, woven design. On the fireplace mantel, she'd tilted an antique beveled mirror picked up at the This and That Shop, a variety store in town. Beside the fireplace, she'd tucked a sizable, lush fern into a wicker basket, and a fabric-covered box near the piano hid an overflow of music.

Someday, she'd purchase her own place and decorate it exactly the way she preferred. But for now, since it was December, she'd draped a green garland along the mantel and added a splash of red spray paint to pinecones arranged in a clear glass bowl on her kitchen counter. On Christmas Eve, she'd set up a spindly artificial tree, then attend the six o'clock church service in Snowflake.

She made a note to herself to purchase a new tree topper. The year before, the previous one had shattered.

And then would come Christmas Day.

Since her divorce she'd spent it alone, a prospect she never looked forward to.

To chat about her eventful evening at the shelter, she phoned Aunt Clementine, who answered on the second ring.

"Hello, Holly," her aunt said. "Is anything the matter?"

"No, why?" Holly bit into her toast and chewed.

"You don't usually call me twice in one day."

"Are you busy?"

"A little."

Holly went along with her aunt, assuming she was joking. Typically at this hour she was snuggled on her flowered recliner watching her favorite game show, a rescue dog or two nestled at her feet.

"I called to tell you that this was easier than I imagined," Holly said.

"What was easier?"

Holly smiled. "How best to use the fifteen hundred dollars Charity gave me. I found a special charitable cause."

"That's the way the Lord works. Don't wear yourself out looking for something that God will place right in front of you."

A muted male voice resounded through the phone.

"Is anyone with you?" Holly asked.

Silence for a beat.

"Aunt Clementine?"

"Justin Kildred is here." Her aunt cleared her throat. "We're watching a game show together."

"The man who volunteered in the reception area the day you were admitted?" A vision of the portly elderly man with wiry white hair and a friendly, hearty chuckle, prompted Holly to smirk.

"The very same. While I was in the hospital, he came to my room and visited me, and before I was discharged, he asked for my number. He told me it took him a few days to gather up his courage to ask me out."

"And she was worth the wait," Justin called out in the background.

Holly gaped into the phone. "When did this all happen?"

"We went on our first date soon after you left, a celebration because of the good report I received from the doctor. And Justin brought me a bouquet of white roses. You know how much I love flowers. And white roses signify new beginnings."

"How romantic." Holly chuckled. "And more important, I'm thrilled about how quickly you convalesced."

"My faith is my greatest report, for God always puts us in the best place for our needs."

"Which includes placing you in the hospital so you could meet Justin?" Holly envisioned her aunt blushing like a sixteen-year-old girl. "You never spoke about him once during all our recent phone conversations."

"I figured you were heartbroken over losing your friend and needed the chance to talk about your friendship."

"Charity wouldn't want us to grieve, although I can't help myself." With a choked laugh, Holly curved her hand across Butterscotch's back and was rewarded with a low purr. "She wished everyone a long and happy life."

"Maybe God was bringing forth new life in her wishes," Aunt Clementine quietly said. "His timing is always perfect."

New life. New beginnings.

Her aunt was finally finding love, and Christmastime made it even more special. She'd lived her entire life alone, and she certainly hadn't been looking for love. But so what? Love at any age was praiseworthy.

Holly picked up Charity's letter and clutched it close to

her chest. It was tear-stained and raveled at the corners. Through Charity, God had given Holly and her friends an assignment. Surely God would see them through and provide assistance.

"Tell me about your special cause," her aunt prompted.

"It all happened so quickly." Holly set down the letter, wrapped her fingers snugly around her mug, and took a sip of the earthy chamomile tea. Then she explained what had happened at the shelter and her conversation with Tim. "Perhaps I'll use the fifteen hundred dollars to find a place for Jasmine and her mother, Emily, to stay."

"How long will that amount last to cover their rent?"

"Only a few months."

"So what about the other people at the shelter?" her aunt asked quietly.

"You're right." With a sigh, Holly set down her mug. "Of course that isn't the best use for the money. I considered donating it to the shelter for the rewiring, but I'm certain that money wouldn't even come close to the required amount."

"Then start a fund-raiser to make up the difference."

"Like what, for instance? A bake sale?"

"You're a musician, aren't you?" Holly visualized her aunt —the lines in her face, the caring heart that held infinite wisdom. "Ask your students to perform a holiday piano recital and solicit donations at the door."

"And where would I hold this recital?" Holly reached for a blank piece of notepaper and a pen she always kept close by. "The wintry weather is unpredictable for an outside performance."

"Why don't you talk to that building inspector and throw around your ideas? What's his name?"

"Tim Stewart." The memory of his tousled brown hair and deep, velvety voice when he apologized for being forced to close the shelter, had a curious effect on Holly's heartbeat.

"Surely he can refer you to an electrician," her aunt said. "Or that other man ... Lou. Can he help?"

"I tried to talk with Lou after I spoke with Jasmine and Emily, but he brushed me off. A few minutes later, he announced he was coming down with the flu and left. He suggested speaking with his assistant, which I did."

"And?"

"He was chatty but useless." Holly scribbled on the notepad, then fixated on her pen. "Basically, he encouraged me to do whatever I want, declaring all the while that nothing will save the shelter."

"Sounds like he was hardly helpful." Her aunt pushed out a heavy sigh. "So, find out where Tim's office is located. He's your guy."

Her guy? Hah! Not if Holly wanted a man who truly cared about helping people instead of displacing them.

"Tim didn't seem inclined to offer a solution," she said.

"What about dating him?" A whisper of mirth from her aunt kept pace with Justin's low belly laugh.

"Date him?" Holly sat up straighter. "Why? I've created a happy life here in Pine Cone Valley. I love my students and music and—"

Even as she refuted her aunt, the word swirled in her brain. *Dating.*

She put the phone on speaker, padded to the piano and braced her hands on the fall board. Dating was for others, not for her.

But how many years had she dreamed about having someone love her, an amazing guy she could love in return? A man to share her life with.

No, no, no. Tim was the bad guy, and she'd married one bad guy.

"I'm not the Grinch who stole Christmas, if that's what's holding you back," he'd said.

Holly went to the couch and plucked up her list, blank save for the scribbles.

Picking up the pen, she wrote while saying aloud, "I'm waiting until God makes it clear I've made the right choice in finding someone extraordinary."

"You should start going out and experiencing life again. You haven't dated since your divorce."

"I'm far from a hermit, Aunt Clementine." Holly drew in a quiet breath. "I'm just not interested, that's all."

"Two years is a long time."

"I'm not desperate, and I won't date a guy who throws homeless women and children onto the street."

"He's hardly done that, dear. And may I remind you that you said he apologized. Tomorrow is Friday. Go see him. From what you've described, he's eager to help."

"He's the opposite of eager."

"Interested then. Let's just say he's interested."

Her aunt didn't elaborate, and Holly didn't press her. A half dozen times, her mind quarreled that she should tell Aunt Clementine about Tim Stewart being an actor—and that he was ruggedly appealing and charismatic. But her aunt hadn't remarked on his name being recognizable, although, in all fairness, she was probably preoccupied with Justin.

The prospect of their romance made Holly smile.

Justin and Aunt Clementine were proving that it was never too late to find love.

CHAPTER FIVE

The following morning, Holly dressed in a turtleneck sweater and formfitting jeans, then tugged on her coat and snagged her leather bucket handbag over her shoulder. Instead of a wool beanie, she fitted a pair of leopard earmuffs over her ears and freshly washed hair.

Brisk air embraced her as she exited her apartment. A radiant sun cast sparkles on the icicles, a shiny twinkle on the picturesque landscape of mountains and valleys.

After setting her GPS for the building inspectors' offices in Snowflake, she started her Jeep on the snow-rutted side street, then veered onto the main highway. The road had been plowed, and she drove quickly to Snowflake.

The day's piano lessons didn't begin until early evening, which allowed time to brainstorm solutions with Tim. Or so she hoped.

When she reached his office, she parked at the curb. A plain boxwood wreath was fixed to the entry door, and Holly envisioned attaching pinecones, red berries, and moss, so that the holiday colors would be highlighted. She'd always had a flair for decorating.

In the office foyer, she inhaled a mixture of old cigarette smoke, a flowery fragrance, and stale coffee.

A receptionist sat behind an oversized mahogany desk and greeted her. The woman looked like she'd done everything she could to fight the aging process—tightening her face with plastic surgery, dying her hair a garish red, and applying a pair of thick black false eyelashes. The result made her appear older, not younger.

"Timothy Stewart, please," Holly said.

"He's out on a call." The woman squinted up at Holly over pink reading glasses. "Do you have an appointment?"

"No. I met him last evening at the homeless shelter and wished to talk to him about my—"

"Henry, Tim's assistant is here," the receptionist interrupted. "Do you want to see him instead?"

"Certainly." At least, Holly thought, there was someone in the office.

The receptionist ushered Holly down the hall and pointed to a tiny cubicle.

Henry, with thinning hair dyed an iridescent purple, offered Holly a seat across from the messiest desk she'd ever seen.

"I heard about the homeless shelter, but I'll try to reach Tim for you as he's more familiar with the problem." Henry punched a number into his cellphone and kept up a stream of one-sided conversation. "I grew up in New York City, but wanted the tranquility of a small town so I relocated here. Did you know that New York has a population of over eight million?"

"That's a hefty percentage in comparison to—"

"Then I went through a complicated divorce and—" He set down the phone. "Tim isn't picking up."

"Well, thanks, anyway." Holly stood before he could begin his nonstop chatter again. "At least you tried. I'll come back after lunch." She slung her handbag over her shoulder and headed into the hallway, spotting a memorable broad-shouldered man with dark wavy hair. Tim's cheeks were reddened from the outside air, which only enhanced his chiseled good looks.

"Miss Kim. What a delightful surprise." An enigmatic smile swept across his face as he surveyed her, from the top of her earmuffs to the toes of her brown leather boots. He carried a cup of steaming coffee in one hand and his gloves in the other. "The receptionist said you were here to discuss the homeless shelter." He checked his watch. "But you should have made an appointment."

"This was spur of the moment and ..." Holly trailed off. He was obviously preoccupied. "Can you spare a few minutes?"

"For you? Certainly. Come into my office." He grinned and gestured to a door down the hall. "I assume you don't want coffee, since it's almost noon. You only drink coffee in the morning, right?"

"Your memory is outstanding."

"I've been told that before, but I'll let you in on a secret. I remember only certain things ... or certain people." He lifted his cup. "Can I get you anything?"

"I'm fine, thanks."

He flashed another grin and she was surprised by its warmth. She recalled that same devastating grin when it had spun across countless television screens, bringing up the heat level of every woman who'd watched him. But after a couple seasons, he'd abruptly left the business and disappeared.

So, he'd decided to settle in Snowflake to become a ... building inspector?

Rather than guessing his reasons for leaving a lucrative acting profession, she inched into his outdated paneled office and met his steady gaze.

He nudged the door closed behind them, set his coffee and gloves on a narrow dilapidated desk that had seen better days, then pulled out a chair for her. Papers were piled high, and half-empty coffee cups furthered the clutter.

He removed his parka, scarf and wool cap. His wrinkled, white button-down shirt strained across his muscled chest.

"Well, Miss Kim?" He slid into a chair behind his desk.

She wiped her sweaty palms on her coat, because for some reason she was nervous about being alone with him. He was, after all, an attractive man with impressively innate appeal. Nevertheless, her expectations had been high when she'd set out for Snowflake this morning.

Now she wasn't so sure. Now she was considering that their discussion might be unsuccessful at best and exasperating at worst.

She took a quick glimpse out the window. Tailor-suited men and women emerged from the entrances of multistory buildings, fastening their down coats and shoving fleece-gloved hands deep into their pockets. Even in this commercial part of town, dense pine wreaths trimmed with red bows decorated the businesses' steel doors. In Snowflake, the spirit of Christmas reached everywhere.

She glanced back at Tim. He stared at her intently, as if waiting for something.

"Well?" he repeated, folding his hands together.

Today he was all business. She sensed his standoffishness and couldn't understand why. Surely she'd done nothing to offend him since she'd entered his office.

She presented a level look. "Well what?"

"Miss Kim—"

"Holly."

"Holly, you're here at *my* workplace, so what can I do for you?" That velvety voice resembling a silky caress had changed to abrupt and businesslike.

In order for their meeting to go forward, she needed to speak, she told herself.

She swallowed. "The shelter needs our help."

"Ah, I see. The shelter needs *our* help." He glanced at his watch again. "Go on."

"There are countless ways to assist." She ignored his impatience with a good-natured smile. "I've brainstormed ideas with my aunt."

"And your aunt is—"

"My aunt Clementine," she flipped back. "She lives in North Carolina and we chat often. I try to visit her whenever I can."

"So your aunt is some sort of homeless shelter expert?"

"She's just my sweet, elderly aunt."

In the ensuing silence, his gaze slid to her mouth. Then he pushed out a deep sigh. "Therefore, you're not here to accept my offer for a date?"

Absolutely not was on the tip of her tongue, warring with an *absolutely yes.*

As her throat went dry, she reined in the enticing thought of actually going out with him.

A date ... with Timothy Stewart. At the same moment that the thought went through her mind, her heart thumped an erratic beat. She was in close quarters with him in his ten by twelve foot office, and the air was scented with leather and the outdoors—purely masculine scents.

She sensed there was an inordinate amount of life that he'd experienced beneath that handsome exterior, and for some reason, he'd sealed all of it behind a barrier of polite courteousness.

Besides, he was far beyond her reach. And she suspected he believed he was beyond God's reach as well.

She wanted to reassure him that God wasn't looking for perfection, and that Tim had made mistakes along with everyone else. God looked for people who were unsure of the next turn, not those who thought they knew it all and were full of their own knowledge.

Her fingers tightened.

So when it came to dating him?

Bad idea. The absolute worst idea.

Besides, she had a history of making poor choices with men, seeing the virtuous and never the unscrupulous. This had led her to marry a narcissistic man who cared only about what she could, or rather, *should,* do for him.

"I told you, Tim, I don't date." She managed a wavering smile. "As I mentioned, I'm here because of the shelter."

For a split second, disappointment flew across his rugged face.

He shrugged indifferently as his blasé mask slid back into place. "Did your visit with Jasmine and her mother go satisfactorily after I left the shelter?"

"As well as it could, considering the circumstances."

Along with a long-suffering look, he sighed. "Not my fault."

"I didn't say it was."

"Good, and Jasmine is an adorable child, by the way."

"She's quite out of the ordinary compared to other students," Holly replied. "For instance, she's mastered two-octave scales, both hands together. Her musicality is incredible for a child who practices only three times a week on an ancient upright piano in Snowflake's only music store."

"Encourage her to stick with it," Tim said. "Music can enhance verbal memory."

"How do you know that?"

"I've read articles, but my knowledge is all second-hand experience."

"Also important to remember is that when you play an instrument, you use both sides of your brain." Holly tried to sound human and not like a page out of a textbook. "I gather you don't play, Tim?

"I play the radio." He grinned and stretched out his long legs beneath the desk. "Other than that, I truly have no musical proficiency."

"You never had the opportunity?"

"That's one way to sum up my childhood. One sugary, polite way." The jaded drawl in his voice, his response immediate and conclusive, told her there was more, but she didn't pressure him.

Their brief cordiality floundered as Holly returned to the subject of the shelter and how to help the residents who were about to be turned out into the cold.

"They won't be 'turned out into the cold,'" Tim said curtly. "To begin with, the various lodgings in the area are willing to assist temporarily." He lifted the coffee to his lips and grimaced, muttering, "I forgot my three sugars." He set the cup to the side.

"Temporarily isn't the right answer," Holly said.

"*Temporarily* will have to do."

"It's a Band-Aid." Holly blew out a breath. She wasn't here to argue with him. "I'm assuming you can direct me to an electrician, the first rung in solving the problem. Do you have anyone in mind? I'm willing to help financially."

Understanding seemed to dawn, and Tim quirked a dark eyebrow. "Really? How?"

"A dear friend recently passed. Her name was Charity. She left money to me and several of our high school friends and tagged it for a good cause. This is certainly the case with the shelter needing all new electrical wiring." Holly struggled to stave off unanticipated hot tears. Wasn't grief supposed to subside with time? Would it never go away?

Tim's expression changed, the strain in his face replaced by compassion. He got to his feet and reached across the desk, touching her shoulders with both hands. "I'm sorry. Charity must have been young. My condolences for your loss."

"I take comfort from a sermon from Pastor Tom I heard a while back."

"Do you?"

"We must endure today's sadness. Remember, a blessed tomorrow is just around the bend." Holly wiped her eyes and repaid Tim's cool tone with a proud reply. "Charity wanted to strengthen her friends during her weakest hours by the gift of generosity."

Belatedly, Holly registered his unreadable expression. "What?"

He dropped his hands. "You won't appreciate my answer."

"Try me."

"I've attended church, and it didn't work for me. I found the people there were judgmental and insincere."

"Then try again."

"No."

His flat reply reminded her of the teenage rebellions she'd dealt with when her adolescent students refused to take piano lessons, but were being forced to by their parents. "Why not?"

"Because I have an aversion to artificiality," he replied. "Which is one of the reasons I'm not in Hollywood anymore."

If Charity were alive, she would encourage Tim to embrace the season of Christ's birth with joy and church attendance. But Charity wasn't here anymore.

Holly drew a fortifying breath in a futile attempt to stave off more tears. She missed her friend considerably.

Tim came around his desk. "Holly—"

There was no distance between them now.

"You must think I'm a woman who cries all the time. I

don't usually break down like this. I guess I'm not as strong as I should be."

"I sense you're very strong." He cupped his hands on her shoulders. "Whatever your ideas, I'll make them work." The tender sincerity in his tone, coupled with the touch of his fingers, comforted her.

She gulped, and her blurry eyes searched his face. Tim had made an assurance without asking for repayment. She tied this with the realization that she simply believed him. His voice had been sincere, his response heartfelt.

"Thank you."

He gave a last encouraging squeeze, then swung back and settled in his seat.

She groped for a handkerchief in her handbag. This weeping must stop, she scolded herself. Charity would want her friends and family to move on with their lives.

"So you're not some rich model with millions of dollars to spare?" he asked teasingly. "Because you're extraordinarily beautiful."

"I'm certainly well past the age to start modeling." She focused on his coffee cup, the coffee he'd hardly touched. "Is that a compliment, by the way?"

He didn't miss a beat. "Actually, it was. Genuine and sincere."

Her cheeks grew hot. Had he also been genuinely sincere when he'd asked her out?

Frustrated by the direction of her musings, she chastised herself. How could she contemplate dating him when she was in the middle of mourning her friend's death and worrying about Jasmine and her mother's calamitous circumstances?

Tim observed her closely. "Holly?"

"To be clear, I assume fifteen hundred dollars isn't adequate for the shelter's rewiring." She tucked her lace handkerchief back into her handbag and placed the bag beneath her chair. "However, my aunt and I discussed a fund-raiser."

"Your lovable aunt Clementine." He smiled. "Let me guess, you're planning a bake sale?"

"No." Holly stifled a discomfited laugh. "Instead, my piano students and I will present a holiday recital and accept donations at the door."

"Are they any good?"

"Who?" she asked innocently. "My students?"

"Yes." He reached for his coffee.

"Well, they're not professionals, although they're extremely diligent."

He took a swallow of coffee, grimaced again, and slid the cup to the farthest spot of his desk. "Are you a hard taskmaster, Holly?" He kept his features straight for a moment before he chuckled.

"I'm not here to describe my teaching methods." She met his chuckle with one of her own. "What's more important is that my students' parents and friends will support the performance, and I expect the community will rally as well."

"And you'll also perform?"

"I usually don't, but I could."

"I'd pay to see you. You could end the program with a Christmas song."

"How about a sing-along?" she asked.

"Even better. I bet you're excellent."

Her pulse jumped at his enthusiasm. Nonetheless, she reminded herself that he'd acted for a living. "I'm okay. I studied music at a distinguished university in New York."

"I presume you have a shiny black grand piano in your home."

"On the contrary, I have a spinet piano in my apartment that works just fine. Someday, I'd like to learn how to play the accordion. The instruments are similar."

"Miss Holly Kim, you grow more interesting by the second." He rolled up his shirt sleeves and fixed her with a direct look. "Where will you hold this recital?"

"How about Golden Birch Manor on Cedar Lane?"

"The senior residents will love it." He rummaged through the top drawer of his desk. Extracting a stack of business cards, he handed her one. "Here's Ralph's information. He's the electrician I recommend, so let's start with getting a cost estimate for the rewiring. By the way, Ralph recently erected a neon sign for the new ice skating rink in town."

"And that's why you recommend him?"

"He's fully qualified and the best in the area. We've been friends a long time."

"If he can erect a neon sign, then clearly he can rewire a homeless shelter," she said humorously.

A neon sign. That was exactly the sign she needed from God, pointing to the right guy before she fell in love again. Inwardly, she shook her head. As if that would ever happen.

What? The neon sign or the guy?

Both, she decided.

"Are you familiar with the rink?" Tim asked. The aloofness was gone, any former brusqueness in his tone subdued.

"I've driven past on many occasions, but I've never ice-skated before."

"You should try sometime. It's fun."

"Fun if you can stand upright on skates," she hedged. "I probably wouldn't even make it to the rink without falling."

He raised his eyebrows in a dare. "I'll hold you up."

She flushed, speechless. A vision of him and her ice-skating together, laughing, the sounds of smooth blades gliding across the ice, the enticing scents of nachos and popcorn from the concession stand, ignited an expectant warmth in her chest.

She gave herself a resolved mental shake. Talk about a

fantasy. Most likely, her ankles would wobble, while he would make skating appear fluid and effortless.

"If you ever want to learn, let me know." It seemed like he wanted to prolong their conversation, and she sat back in her chair while he continued. "I played hockey on two high school teams."

"You attended more than one high school?"

"I attended five."

"Why so many?"

"My mother and I constantly moved around." His eyes darkened, and he looked away.

"I assume this was all before you became an actor?"

He raked a hand through his hair. "I've been on my own for most of my life, and spent several years in a variety of professions, yet that's the one everyone brings up. Thankfully, that stint is long past."

Abruptly, he stood, a firm conclusion. Their meeting was apparently over.

Holly scooped up her handbag. "Shall I call the electrician?"

"I'll text Ralph to arrange a discussion." Tim tugged his phone from his pocket. After quick back-and-forth texts, he read, "He can meet at the town center on Saturday, December seventh, the night of the tree-lighting ceremony. He's slated to be there in case anything goes wrong."

"Like if the tree doesn't light up?"

"Something like that."

"I haven't been to a tree lighting in ages, but I remember it was always held the first Saturday in December." She hadn't been since she'd gone with Charity and their friends when they were in high school.

"Neither have I." Tim studied her and smiled, and she had the most surprising thought. He seemed to definitely be admiring her. "So, we can all plan to meet there."

"*All?*"

"I'll come too," he said. "What's your phone number?"

Did she have a choice? It seemed as if he'd asked numerous times already. She offered her number, he put it into his phone, and then her phone pinged with a text. It was from Tim.

Five o' clock on December 7th? he'd texted. *I'll meet you in front of The Little Corner Bistro in Snowflake on Main Street. Ralph will be with me.*

I'll be there, she texted back.

This was absurd. He was standing right across from her and they were texting each other. She looked up at him, and their gazes locked.

And then, the strangest thing happened. They both laughed at the same time.

CHAPTER SIX

A few days after meeting with Tim, Holly's thoughts continuously veered back to him—the strength of his fingers on her shoulders, his rich chuckle, his admiring smile. Everything about him melted her into an illogically thinking female. How could a man like him possibly be interested in a woman like her? She'd been told she was pretty, but she certainly didn't parallel a curvaceous starlet.

Surely she was the least stunning woman he'd ever bothered to flirt with. Did he assume he could lure her into a meaningless date with trite, empty flattery?

And then what, after he'd tired of her?

Why, he'd do what her ex had done.

She refused to dwell on the scenario, but had learned from experience.

Tim would abandon her.

At four o'clock on the day of Snowflake's tree-lighting ceremony, Holly gave herself a final once-over in the foyer mirror and smiled. She'd spent an hour getting ready, something she usually never did—opting for black mascara and a touch of blue eyeshadow to complement her dark eyes. Sparingly, she brushed on a light rose blush to her cheekbones, then applied lipstick in a sun-kissed mauve tone. Her reflection smiled back, and she attributed her shining eyes not to her makeup, but because she was seeing Tim.

She tucked her hair beneath a wool cap, and knotted a sumptuous blue cashmere scarf over her coat.

Snow had begun to fall when Holly stopped at the motel that was temporarily putting up Jasmine and Emily.

She insisted on bringing them to the tree-lighting.

At first Emily declined, her thin lips flattening, before finally complying for her daughter's sake.

They piled into Holly's car and arrived at the resplendently decorated town center where the unlit tree towered, and Holly snagged a parking space in a lot off Main Street. The town resembled an oil painting of a chocolate-box Christmas scene, enhanced by mouth-watering cocoa beans flavoring the air from Sheila's Gourmet Chocolates.

The dark green of the pines contrasted with their coating of pristine frosty snowflakes. Jasmine's breath left white puffs as she incessantly chattered, and the muted crunch of their boots on the hardened snow assured that the winter season had a firm hold on the town.

As they approached the town center, they marveled at the winking silver lights in the shops' windows, and Holly ducked into the This and That Shop to probe their inventory of antiques before they closed. The observance of Christmas in a modest, Americana Colorado town was a sparkling and detailed affair. At one corner, a flashing red arrow pointed to Candy Cane Avenue, a side alley lined with candy canes.

"It even smells like peppermint!" Jasmine exclaimed, and the women smilingly echoed her enthusiasm.

At the end of the avenue the humane society had organized an 'adopt a dog' event. Multiple dogs wearing white-and-red velvet Santa hats chased an inflatable ball in a fenced-in area, while miniature piles of puppies, resting on each other, barked playfully and looked on.

Jasmine's cherubic face beamed, and she tugged at Emily's coat sleeve. "Can we adopt a puppy, Mommy? I always wanted a shih tzu."

"Maybe someday. And older dogs need companions too." Emily replied with cautious deliberation, which Holly attributed to an abundance of broken dreams. "Once we get back on our feet and have our own place, we'll see."

"That will happen," Holly encouraged.

"Will it?" Emily invariably had such a faraway stare. "It's difficult being a single parent, and I'm all alone."

"Not anymore. I'm here to help you." Holly offered an upbeat nod of confirmation. "In fact, the entire community is. Look at how the town rallied and found space for everyone."

As they proceeded, Emily declined Holly's offer of money so Jasmine could buy some hot chocolate or little trinkets. Respecting the woman's wishes, Holly placed her wallet back inside her handbag.

What made people too proud to accept a kindness, despite desperate circumstances? Didn't they realize it was a joy to give? Charity had often quoted a favorite Bible verse, 2 Corinthians 8:12: "For if the willingness is there, the gift is acceptable according to what one has, not according to what one does not have."

"Okay," Holly said. "But if you change your mind ..."

Emily twisted the cheap wristwatch around her skinny wrist and didn't answer. Holly had the urge to place her hand over the woman's, calming the anxious gesture.

Farther down the street, they ducked in and out of local shops and grinned at holiday shoppers sipping mulled wassail. Jasmine inhabited her own little space, taking it all in—the fruity scents of apples, lemons, and oranges mingling with cinnamon.

Seasonal markets clustered together selling residents' handicrafts. Spotting a unique stand, Jasmine tugged them over to a craft booth where an older woman was making homemade dolls. Traditional and beguiling, each doll was designed with a whimsical smile.

The woman used coffee-brown colored yarn to knot two eyes, then cut out a heart-shaped piece of red felt for the mouth.

"I loved dolls when I was young, but now I'm too old for them." Jasmine sighed and cupped a tiny doll lovingly. She handled the thick braids of yarn and dashed her fingers along the doll's gingham dress, circling the wide white buttons.

"You're never too old if it's something you love," Holly said. "The fact that you appreciate a beautifully handcrafted doll means you're imaginative and artistic. Which we already recognize, of course." Holly and Emily exchanged a smile. "Because you're a quick learner."

Beaming, Jasmine drummed her fingers on the counter as she leaned in to inspect the other dolls.

"Please let me buy this doll for you." Holly immediately noted Emily's frown and chided herself for not asking her permission first.

Jasmine jumped up and down. "Please, Mommy?"

Emily's face filled with regret. She surveyed the doll, then her daughter. Finally, her silver-gray eyes met Holly's. "Are you sure, Miss Kim?"

"It's my pleasure and we'll call it an early holiday gift," Holly said. "Agreed?"

"Yay, yay yay!" Jasmine snuggled the doll close to her chest. "Thank you, Miss Kim." The elation in the child's eyes was a reflection of the true spirit of Christmas.

"This gift gives *me* more happiness than you can ever imagine," Holly said.

A chill was in the air, and the scent of fire-roasted chestnuts permeated every inch of space. Food trucks sold homemade candy, and Holly was drawn to Nancy's Caramel Station, selling delectable, buttery caramels. She bought a half pound and shared the candies with her companions. The caramels were dense and chewy, a gooey delight.

The magical holiday atmosphere was furthered by evergreen wreaths twined with eucalyptus leaves and emerald satin ribbons placed uniformly on each shop door. The distinctive woodsy scent unmistakably proclaimed Christmas.

"I don't recall the tree lighting being anywhere near as wonderful when I was younger," Holly murmured.

"Life's defining stages." Emily's hands flew through her thin hair, and her severe features relaxed. "I read about it in my self-improvement book. Each stage you're in gives you a different perspective of the world."

"See, Mommy. I told you tonight would be fun." Jasmine supplied a tooth-filled grin and wiped a glob of caramel stuck to the edge of her mouth. "Let's go visit the dogs!"

"You two run along," Holly attempted to keep the jump of excitement from her tone. "It's almost time for me to meet the building inspector."

Emily removed her square-framed glasses and polished the lenses with the sleeve of her drawstring jacket. "You're meeting the bad guy here tonight, Miss Kim?"

Holly bristled, immediately coming to Tim's defense. "The shelter's defective wiring isn't his fault, and he's working with me and a host of others to get it fixed. I'll catch up with you two afterwards."

"Sounds good. C'mon, Mommy!" Jasmine quickly ended the women's verbal duel. "See you later, Miss Kim."

A chorus of brass instruments—several of Snowflake High

School's band students playing the tuba, trombone, and trumpet—rang a medley of well-loved carols with "It Came Upon a Midnight Clear," succeeded by a jubilant "God Rest Ye, Merry Gentlemen."

Meanwhile, other members of the band played under the gazebo, and the melodies brought a grin to Jasmine's pale face as she raced off with her mother in tow.

Armed with an animated smile, Holly reached The Little Corner Bistro a few minutes later. She lingered, mesmerized by the tiny candles illuminating each window. Assorted restaurants were open, and patrons wearing sleek parkas with fur-trimmed hoods perused the outdoor menus. Scents of flame-grilled meats melded with basil and garlic, beckoning them inside.

Women idled as they passed the bistro, feasting their eyes on Tim.

Which was how Holly spotted him, as he reigned tall and straight and unbearably handsome outside the bistro. Because of the admiring women.

That, and because his athletic physique filled out his familiar quilted parka flawlessly. His attractive face showed the beginnings of a dark beard.

He was conversing with an older, gruff-looking man wearing thick glasses and a plaid wool coat. Tim tilted his head toward the man, suggesting that he was attending to the conversation, although he examined the crowd as if he was searching for someone.

He was searching for her, Holly thought with an inner tingle.

Seeming to detect her presence, he lifted his head abruptly, and their gazes locked.

Before she'd scanned the crowd a second time, he'd reached her.

"Holly?" He offered his usual charismatic smile, and her

breath caught. "I haven't seen you in what … five days?"

She couldn't stand still and tried to relax her breathing. The magical atmosphere had transformed the night into one of enchantment, especially with a handsome, enigmatic guy at her side.

She stole a peek at him, appreciating the strength carved into his chiseled cheekbones and tanned face. Timothy Stewart was exactly what fairy tale princes were created from —broad-shouldered, hard-working, and compelling.

She bit back a grin. "But you text me all the time."

Since their initial meeting in his office, he'd texted each evening at eight o'clock when she'd finished teaching.

How was your day? he'd always begin.

Jasmine is the most precocious and talented student I've taught in several years, she'd texted back. *I only wish she had a decent piano to practice on, and a parent who was more invested in her progress. I've arranged to give her lessons at a music store in Snowflake.*

Slightly self-conscious by her chatty zeal for Jasmine, Holly described her other piano students and schedule.

Once, when silence lapsed, she'd informed him about how she'd subbed for the pianist at Snowflake Chapel. She'd been tempted to invite him to Sunday service, but didn't. He always brushed off every reference to church, changing the subject to inquire about her aunt or students or her cat.

What is Butterscotch doing? he'd ask, and she'd reply, *Nothing. Lazy, as usual. And your stray kitten?*

He'd confided that he'd revisited the shelter and adopted one of the kittens.

She is company for me, because my place is lonely.

Holly had studied the phone screen. Lonely? Him? What was he trying to tell her?

Hurriedly, she combed her thoughts for another topic but fell short when she failed to think of anything. Finally, she texted, *Have you thought of a good name for your kitten?*

Taffy.

Sweet. For a man who was just as sweet.

As the days progressed, Holly clicked on her cellphone each evening with anticipation and delight.

The previous evening, she'd finished with, *Well, I'm calling it a night. I'll see you tomorrow.*

Can I tell you how much I'm looking forward to it? he'd asked.

Her pulse had given a leap of excitement.

Why?

Because I like talking with you, especially in person.

Calm down, she'd told herself after he'd sent that text.

And she was telling herself the same thing now. They'd arranged this get-together to figure out a solution to the shelter's dilemma. This wasn't about seeing Tim again.

The older man, who must be Ralph, approached, grinning broadly. "So this is the gorgeous lady you've been yakking about." Conspiratorially, he winked at Tim.

"Thanks for keeping my secret," Tim murmured.

"I didn't know it was a secret. Besides, you can't keep a beautiful woman under wraps forever." Ralph kept his unrepentant grin on Holly. "You don't live in Snowflake or I would have recognized you."

"I live in Pine Cone Valley," she answered. "I'm a piano teacher."

"So I heard."

"I teach a girl who lived at the homeless shelter with her mother."

"Jasmine, right?" Ralph quizzed. "She and her mother are staying at the motel in town at a heavily discounted rate until this electrical situation at the shelter is resolved."

"Yes. How did you learn about her?"

"Well, now, I wonder." Ralph sent a teasing look toward Tim, then extended a hand to Holly. "Tim and I go way back. He was such a solemn little boy."

He really had been talking about her to his friends, she thought.

"You're a fountain of information tonight, Ralph," Tim said with an offhand laugh.

She smiled and shook Ralph's hand. "I'm Holly."

"Tim and I have texted the last few days." Ralph reached into his pocket, extracted a folded sheet of paper, and passed it to her. "I stopped by the shelter and the problem isn't as severe as everyone anticipated. But don't forget, the building hasn't been updated in twenty years, and chances are it will require upgrading."

Holly unfolded the paper and scrutinized it. "Three thousand dollars is your repair estimate?"

"Be warned. Rewiring is chaotic, disruptive work. Lou has a copy of my estimate too. It should be accurate, give or take any surprises."

"In this business, there are always surprises," Tim inserted. "So round out that number to thirty-five hundred dollars."

"I'll donate fifteen hundred toward the project," Holly said. "Somehow, we'll make up the difference."

"*We?*" Ralph's smile faded. "I'm working at a reduced rate already."

"I meant me and the business community, and anyone else who wants to contribute," Holly said. "I have various fundraisers in mind."

"Like what?" Ralph countered. "A bake sale?"

Tim and Holly both laughed.

"Private joke," Tim explained.

Mayor Hardy, who prevailed at a podium by the tree, spotted Ralph and waved him over.

From where they stood, Ralph surveyed the tall, unlit pine. "I'll catch up with you two in an hour," he called over his shoulder as he shuffled away.

"I brought Jasmine and Emily with me tonight," Holly said to Tim. "They're over on Candy Cane Avenue with the dogs. I'll meet them after the ceremony."

She regarded the steady stream of shoppers, the beginning of the retail rush. Why was the Christmas season so commercialized? Wasn't the holiday supposed to be a Christian holy day to mark the birth of the Son of God?

"How are they faring?" Tim's quiet tone jerked her from her reflections.

"Moderately well, considering the upheaval of moving into a motel." Holly placed Ralph's estimate into her handbag. "In addition, Emily is applying for a number of jobs this week."

"That's encouraging. I'm optimistic that she'll find a decent position soon." His hand on her elbow, Tim gently drew Holly away from the jam-packed sidewalk.

She glanced up at him. "Where are we going?"

He gestured to an outside seating area serving hot chocolate and tiny, fried cinnamon-glazed doughnuts. Portable heaters and a canvas canopy outfitted with Edison light bulbs created a snug, welcoming atmosphere.

"Do you want to grab something to eat?" he asked. "My treat."

This might be a date. She didn't want to date him. Or did she?

She hesitated.

"Do you prefer somewhere else?" He surveyed the various kiosks, looking like he could easily be hurt by her reply if she refused.

"No, this spot is ideal."

"Good." He guided her to a turquoise-colored bistro table and pulled out a chair for her. She liked that about him—standing until she was seated, always courteous, calm, and considerate.

"It's not exactly quiet, and the menu is limited to beverages and doughnuts," he said. "It's more of a—"

"Everything is lovely. The vintage lights on the awning and the little place selling homespun sweets"—she gestured to the shop across the way—"smells wonderful."

He settled across from her. "So you're not teaching again for a couple days?"

His inquiry won him her astonished gape. "You remembered my text?"

He was so fine looking, and she loved the way he listened to her, honestly listened, as if every word she spoke—or texted—was important.

"I've learned a lot about you because I've been reading your texts over and over."

She tipped her head. "Why would you do something like that?"

His heated scrutiny of her sent her pulse into a double rhythm. "You really have to ask?"

On the tip of her tongue were the words, *Yes, I really do*.

But she really didn't, because that irresistible attraction tugged her ever closer to him.

In an attempt to avoid his searching gaze, she studied the menu as a freckle-faced teenage waitress started toward them.

"Hot chocolate and doughnuts?" Holly asked him.

"Sure."

After the waitress took their orders, Holly leaned back in her chair. "Hot chocolate reminds me of sledding, or simply sitting by a window and watching the snow fall." She smiled. "What about you?"

"Nope." He did the opposite of echoing her enthusiasm by pressing his lips together and grimacing. "Hot chocolate isn't part of my childhood memories."

"Oh, I see."

Although she didn't see anything of the sort.

After they were served the piping hot cocoa laced with whipped cream and yeasty deep-fried doughnuts, Holly bent her head to say grace. Tim supported her lead. Granted, he didn't pray, but he bowed his head.

"Do you always say a blessing before every meal?" he asked when she whispered "amen."

"Absolutely. It's a way to show respect to God, and gratitude for our blessings."

Thoughtfully, he took a sip of hot chocolate. "So, tell me more about your fund-raiser."

"My students are all on board to play piano for the benefit recital." Holly savored a mouthwatering taste of whipped cream, finishing with a bite of her warm doughnut. "Jasmine and I are working on a difficult duet arrangement of 'Silent Night.'"

Tim averted his head. "Duly noted."

"You don't like 'Silent Night'?"

"Everyone likes 'Silent Night.'"

"Is it because you don't like church?"

He shrugged. "Like I said, it's not for me."

"Did you ever attend church?"

"What do I look like, Holly? The Grinch again?"

"Sorry."

"We went, but certainly not often." He picked up a spoon and stirred the hot chocolate in his mug. "While we lived near Denver, we visited my grandparents. When we did, my mother often argued with my grandmother."

"What did you do? I mean, while they argued. You were a little kid."

"My grandfather was a contractor, and he'd bring me along on his jobs. He taught me all about the building trade." Tim raised both his hands and grinned. "And thus, here I am. All that on the job training paid off, plus four years of taking college courses at night, multiple certifications, and passing licensing exams."

"You're a great guy."

"Me?"

She threw him a comic sigh. "You're not as cynical and hardhearted as I first suspected."

"Hmm. Gee, thanks."

"But we were talking about your grandfather."

"He was the best," Tim said quietly. "Unfortunately, there were days when he didn't take me with him and I'd be subjected to a firsthand blow-out between my grandmother and mother. My grandmother would go on and on about church, insisting religion was precisely what my mother needed—a clergyman to set her on a respectable path and enable her to overcome her many addictions."

"Which were?"

"Alcohol, pills, whatever she could get." He hesitated. He couldn't seem to find his words. "As usual, my mother expelled the idea as quickly as my grandmother fired it at her."

"She wasn't in favor of getting help?"

"She wasn't in favor of anything my grandmother suggested. They had a prickly relationship, which is stating it mildly. Grandmother disapproved of my mother's lifestyle, and looking back, I can understand why. My mother only visited when she was out of money."

A silence lapsed as Holly collected her thoughts. Nearby, the brass band launched into a jazzy rendition of "A Holly Jolly Christmas."

"Were you out of money often?" Holly asked.

"What do you think? Let's just say she would have fit in seamlessly during the flower child era. She drove around in a Volkswagen bus with her friends like life was a never-ending party, while I hung out in the back seat."

"How old were you?"

"Eleven, twelve." He reinforced his recollection with an indifferent head shake. "My mother even changed her name from Sally to Astra. As you can imagine, my grandmother wasn't thrilled about that, either."

"Pretty name."

"Astra means star—derived from the star. My mother said it reminded her of Christmas. Ironic, in view of the fact that we didn't celebrate."

"Where is she now?" Holly surveyed his mug and half-eaten doughnut. He'd pushed both to the side.

"She passed away from pneumonia and a hard life." Tim's voice trailed off into silence. "Years ago."

"I'm sorry."

"Thanks." He swallowed hard. "The next day I headed west. I was nineteen when I arrived in Hollywood."

Hollywood at nineteen. A lively discussion about his adventures in that shiny town should have ensued. Instead, Holly felt an unexpected sadness for him.

"Forgive me, Tim." She concentrated on the festivities—youngsters carrying bags of buttery popcorn and skipping backward, their watchful parents close behind. "My questions were too intrusive."

CHAPTER SEVEN

*S*he was right, Tim thought. Her questions, their confidences, brought up painful memories. They'd only known each other a few days, and he'd always kept his personal life off limits. Yet, as she watched him expectantly, he wanted to talk with her in spite of his inner hesitancy, in spite of his vow to never dwell on his childhood.

He inhaled, his memories peeling back fifteen years. "I remember sitting in the passenger seat of a rig after I'd hitchhiked," he said softly.

"Where are you going?" the truck driver had asked.

"Wherever you are," Tim had replied.

"The trucker was driving to Hollywood to drop off some costumes for a movie set. He introduced me around, so I was able to get some work the next few years, doing various odd jobs at the studios and construction. I started auditioning for acting roles too, and even hired an acting coach." Tim shrugged. "Eventually I got a minor role on a TV show. That led to another, and finally I landed a spot on a popular television series."

"Congratulations," Holly said.

He smiled. Nodded.

Way before that, there were the do-gooders, the authorities who threatened to separate Tim from his mother. Sure, as an adult he understood that children should be safeguarded, but as a child, he only wanted to stay with his mother. And because of the fear that he might be taken from her, she often switched into protective mode and avoided appealing to the powers that be for help.

But this was Holly.

Sitting across from her, sharing the celebratory nature of the evening, compelled him to tell her more about himself.

And that was a first for him.

Besides, he wryly reflected, he didn't want to dampen her enthusiasm for their upcoming fund-raising conversation by answering her questions with curtness.

He steepled his hands and leaned forward. "I don't mind. Honestly. Next, I suppose you'll ask me about my father."

"If you'd like to talk, I'm here to listen."

Clad in a crimson-red coat with a thick blue scarf wrapped around her, she was breathtaking—all fresh-faced complexion and enormous eyes framed by thick lashes and gracefully arched eyebrows. Her black hair was tucked beneath a wool cap and a stray wisp fell across her cheek. The glow of the vintage light bulbs highlighted her soft skin and softer, enticing lips.

"Tim?" Holly propped her small chin on her palms, suspending his delightful observation. "Your father?"

"I didn't know him well." His account was lacking, and Tim allowed a pause before continuing. "All my mother used to say is that he ruined her life."

Because she'd had a baby. And she'd named the baby Tim.

Holly slid her hand across the table. "Did your father desert you and your mother?"

"On the contrary, my mother left him." Tim closed his

hand over hers. Holly offered reassurance and comfort, and he decided to accept it. Another first. "My mother was a free spirit. Everything was done her way."

"Where is he now?"

"My father?" Tim tried to smile. "For many years he was absent from my life, and then he reappeared when I was cast in that television series. I suppose he was after money, assuming I was a rich and famous actor." He stared off, noting Ralph chatting with the mayor, the families gathering near the enormous tree.

Holly nodded toward his mug. "Your hot chocolate is getting cold."

He detected sympathy welling in her eyes, although she strove for a heartening smile. She'd clearly caught his distasteful tone at the mention of his father.

He picked up his mug. "I'm sure it's fine."

The last time he drank hot chocolate he'd been in grade school. These days, his likings ran toward a refreshing beer after work. Fearing she would disapprove because she was obviously a churchgoer and his mother had repeatedly lectured that God had strict rules you were supposed to follow, he amplified his sip with a smile. "This is excellent, especially during the Christmas season."

A season he hadn't celebrated in years.

Wait. There was that one Christmas when they'd arrived at his grandparents' house. Or rather, he'd arrived. He'd never been certain where his mother had disappeared to. He only knew that he'd bought her a gift with the money he'd earned working with his grandfather.

He shook his head. Those memories, that gift, were too difficult to deal with, and he shoved them aside, preferring happier reminiscences. His mother had loved him, but if she was pushed, she loved the drink more. Surely by now, he'd accepted that.

And then there were the pleasant emotions, the giddiness of waking up Christmas morning in his grandparents' secure home, despite he and his mother always being despairingly broke.

That remembrance of a happy Christmas gave birth to a heartening possibility; and a chunk of his resistance, the barricade he'd firmly erected from one end of his broken dreams to another, began to split.

Was a real Christmas in the future for him—that elusive spirit of goodwill? Was Christmas about receiving, like the child he'd been as he'd contentedly unwrapped his grandparents' gifts? Or was Christmas truly the season of giving, per Holly's intent?

And was it about God's love and forgiveness, as Christians proclaimed?

He kept his hand around Holly's, studying her lips, rosy from the invigorating air.

"What people don't understand," he said, "is that just because an actor gains a modicum of success doesn't mean he's amassed a fortune. Especially if you give most of it away."

"You gave the money you earned away?"

"Just about." He gentled his reply with a smile. "I didn't make millions, as most assumed. I wasn't the lead in the series. Actually, I got the role of a secondary character when the actor who originally had the part opted to work on a different show."

"So who did you give your money to?"

She didn't seem interested in the amount of money, which surprised him. That was initially the first thing everyone wanted to know.

He focused on the brass band performing a rousing rendition of "The Twelve Days of Christmas" while the crowd chimed in with, "'And a partridge in a pear tree'" at the end of each verse.

Holly toyed with her doughnut, apparently waiting for his reply.

"Who do you guess I gave the money to?" he asked.

"Your father?

"He claimed he was in a jam." Tim gave a derisive snort. "But my grandmother had stated countless times that he was constantly in a jam, which she blamed on compulsive gambling." Tim scrubbed a hand over his face, as if he could rub away the memories of his father's betrayal. "He was supposed to use the money to check into a treatment program. By the time I reached out to see how he was doing, he'd disappeared. I haven't heard from him since."

Tim caught Holly's expression of understanding, the slight slump of her posture, and tugged his hand from hers. He didn't need her sympathy, he cautioned himself. He didn't need anything from anybody. He'd made his own way and had done just fine.

She blinked.

"Holly?"

"Hmm?" Her eyes welled with tears.

"You're crying?" he asked skeptically.

She flapped a dismissive hand. "Don't mind me. I cry when the commercials appear on television about sponsoring an abandoned puppy in a shelter."

"Please don't feel sorry for me." He tipped up her chin. "My mother cared about me and my grandparents were wonderful. I don't have any emotional wounds. I promise."

"You must. Your parents were neglectful, and—"

"No more talk about me or my past." With an indifference he didn't feel, he blew out a breath.

"You're important too Tim."

He dropped his hand. "Let's discuss your fund-raiser, all right?"

"All right." She faltered, then plucked a sheet of notepaper from her handbag. "I consulted the internet and discovered that it's best to start with a name."

"And what name did you come up with?"

"I hadn't decided on any until now, but what about Astra?" She perked up. "Because we're reaching for the stars to create a better and safer shelter."

"No, no." He crossed his arms. "You initially blamed me for the electrical problem, and now you're thinking about naming your fund-raiser after my mother?"

"It's a lovely name and ideal for the season. The star of Bethlehem guided the three wise men, and a star is the glowing symbol of hope."

"Astra. My mother. A star of hope." Tim sucked in a quick breath. "And then what?"

"Then we formulate a plan. But wait. Are you okay with the name?"

He saluted.

"Good."

Her infectious smile, her eagerness, made it challenging to concentrate on their conversation, or take a nibble of his doughnut or a gulp of tepid chocolate. Holly was unabashedly enthusiastic, and her energetic voice captivated him.

He uncrossed his arms, taken aback at how his heart spun in his chest, precisely the same as when he'd first laid eyes on her at the shelter.

"There are state regulations and building permits," he murmured, half to himself. "I'll look into them."

"And I'll solicit the parishioners in my church for donations. They're always generous. Plus, I'm going with the idea of a Christmas sing-a-long at the conclusion."

"Okay." He raised his mug for a toast, feeling slightly foolish for his youthful excitement. "What about a tree decorating? Ask the attendees to contribute money, plus bring an ornament to hang on a Christmas tree."

"I like that." Deliberately, she nodded. "But where is this tree? There was a pine at the shelter, and Jasmine and the other children trimmed it before they left."

A Christmas tree. He'd never hung ornaments on a tree before, not even at his grandparents' house.

"We'll set up a tree at the nursing home. I'll donate it." He took her hand, drawing the shape of a pine tree on her palm with his thumb.

He feasted his gaze on her glistening eyes, her ready smile. Could she truly be genuine and so different from the do-gooders he'd dealt with when he and his mother were home-less? Individuals who claimed they would help, but did so only for publicity?

"I phoned the Golden Birch Manor, and the director said she is thrilled to support us." Holly lifted her face, shim-mering with delight. "The residents will enjoy hearing the students play holiday carols, and the facility will place the donation box at the entrance."

He squeezed her hand in encouragement. "Thank you for sharing your vision with me. You're an inspiration."

"Because this is my vision and my mission," she declared, with a satisfied wag of her head. "I've scheduled the recital date for December twenty-third at three o'clock, which gives me a little over two weeks to raise the funds. Will Ralph allow the shelter any leeway if he doesn't receive the full payment when the work is completed?"

"He's a hard man to get to know, but once you do, you'll discover he's good-hearted," Tim replied. "Though I can't predict what he'll say because he must pay his employees too."

"I'll donate my fifteen hundred dollars immediately, and that should move things quicker." He was aware she looked to him for a smile to soothe her unspoken concerns. He obliged, then stated he was ready to render assistance to Ralph and the shelter, and that he was well-connected to the community because of his job. Moreover, her fund-raiser seemed feasible.

"I'd like all the residents to move back by New Year's Eve," she said.

"That will make for a happy New Year?"

"A very happy New Year."

"Attention." The mayor's microphoned voice boomed, accompanied by a drum roll from the band's percussionist. "Our very own Snowflake High School chorus is singing Christmas carols by candlelight, and the tree-lighting ceremony begins in fifteen minutes."

"Ready?" Tim checked the time on the town clock. At Holly's affirmation, he signaled for the check and paid the bill. As they rose, he took her hand as if it was the most natural thing in the world.

She stalled when they passed a candy stand. "I'd like to buy Jasmine a bagful of caramels. She loves them."

"Whenever you mention her, your face lights up," Tim said. "And being well-acquainted with Mayor Hardy's fondness for speech-making, I guarantee there's plenty of time."

"I feel a love for Jasmine that's difficult to explain."

He chuckled at her sincere smile, then gestured toward the candy stand. "Will you buy candy for me too?"

"I suppose I can spare you some." She purchased two separate pounds and provided him with his own bag.

"You're a generous woman, Holly." He popped a caramel into his mouth, offered her one, then shepherded her to a quiet area behind the crowd. "This spot is just right."

"We can't see the tree lighting from back here."

"We will once the tree is lit."

"Shouldn't we move closer?"

"I can't imagine why, when here is perfectly fine." He leaned against a tree trunk and nestled her in his arms.

"Jasmine and her mother are here." Holly squirmed and

went up on her tiptoes. "I told them I would meet them afterwards to bring them back to their motel. I pray that her mother—"

"If she's struggling with an addiction, she'll need support. The shelter offers excellent resources, and seeking a job is admirable."

She prompted him to look toward a booth selling beverages—bottled water and warm cider and soft drinks.

"They don't serve alcohol at these events, Holly."

"It's just that ... I would do anything for that little girl."

"So you mentioned." Tim scanned the crowd. "I don't see them and the ceremony hasn't started yet, so they're probably playing with the dogs on Candy Cane Avenue and it's all good."

"Maybe we should—"

"Holly." He inclined his head and brushed a kiss on her temple, his lips gliding down her cheek and settling on her mouth for a kiss. "Thank you."

She drew back. "Why?"

"Because you are kind and determined and thoroughly gorgeous." He smoothed his hands across her cheeks to lighten the moment before he recognized that the look in her glistening gaze wasn't confusion. She felt the same tug of emotion that he did.

"I should get another bagful of candy for Jasmine before the stand closes, and—"

He grinned, not intending to change his plans in the least.

"Tim? Did you hear what—"

"Holly." Again, he touched her lips with his, exquisitely gentle. "Let's stop talking."

CHAPTER EIGHT

*S*he must have dined at the Cozy Coffee Shop a dozen times, Holly thought as she snagged one of the few empty tables, tucked by the entrance. Invariably, she appreciated the comfortable interior—sunny and lively with light-colored walls and a splash of brilliant-red poinsettias decorating each table—and detected the aroma of freshly ground coffee beans and the daily baked baguettes. A rolling jazzy arrangement of Christmas music played softly in the background.

Tim strode to the table and set down their tray. "Eggnog latte and a peppermint brownie for lunch?" He raised his eyebrows.

"Technically, eleven thirty is still morning." She smoothed down her red V-neck velour sweater that matched her red slacks as she defended her choices, which were startlingly lacking in nutrition. Unapologetically, she inspected his plate. "Should I have ordered your selections? Double smoked-bacon on a croissant and a cup of black coffee?"

"What's wrong with it?"

"Black coffee cancels out the calories of a buttery crois-sant and bacon?"

Amusement flicked over his features. "If you recall, I take my coffee with three sugars, so there goes your calorie-counting theory."

She took a swallow of latte—steamed eggnog, dark-brewed espresso, and a dash of cinnamon. "You should try to look a little embarrassed by your choice of food groups."

"I will if you will," he teased in response. When he smiled, his eyes crinkled up at the corners, flashing with wit and keen intellect.

The same overheating of her senses she'd experienced the night of the tree-lighting ceremony flooded through her. She avoided his gaze and focused on his navy-blue parka as he hung it on a rack beside her coat.

"I'm paying for lunch," she reminded him, "because you treated last time."

"That's why I ordered the early luncheon special, to save you money," he teased. "In fact, I might order the daily dessert too. Muffins are half price on Saturdays."

"Be my guest," she said graciously. "But first, let's say grace." She bent her head. Tim didn't participate, but he kept his head bowed until she completed the prayer.

The shop's glass door swung open heralding a burst of wind, casually teasing his thick, dark hair. Thick and rich and the color of root beer, she decided. His hair was styled to lay flat on the sides, fairly long at the nape, the waves sweeping against his shirt collar. Over his shirt, he wore a fisherman knit sweater.

She sampled her brownie and briefly closed her eyes to savor the sweetness of mint chocolate laced with peppermint buttercream icing. "It's delightful. Do you want a bite?"

"Only if you let me pay for lunch." He slid onto the seat across from her so that their knees touched.

"I told you—"

"It's the least I can do to thank you for your commitment to the homeless shelter."

"You mean the Astra project," she corrected.

"My mother wasn't exactly the poster child for Christmas." Wryly, he smiled. "And may I point out that we were talking about lunch and concluded with my refusal to allow you to pay?"

"Tim, you agreed to let me treat today."

"I don't recall ever actually agreeing." His dark eyes glinted with mischief. "In any case, I changed my mind."

"Are you the persistent type who won't quit badgering me until I agree?"

"I'm known for being extremely tenacious, especially if I want something." The serious tone of his voice robbed her of any retort, and she avoided his roguish expression by staring at the poinsettia.

She'd been thrilled when he'd suggested meeting at the coffee shop, hoping all week that he'd ask her out. And with that hope, she'd questioned herself.

What was she doing? These feelings, these rose-colored glasses, were completely out of character. She'd sworn off men after her unpleasant experience with her ex.

"A bite of your brownie?" he repeated. "Or do you intend to eat it all by yourself?"

Obligingly, she offered him a nibble.

"Just like I imagined." He laced his fingers through hers. "Delicious."

A hazardous warmth invaded Holly's bloodstream. Warily, she lifted her hand from his.

In the days since the tree lighting, she'd taught a full schedule of daily piano lessons, and Tim had put in a seventy-hour workweek. Still, he'd texted or called nightly, and they'd compared notes on the progress of the fund-raiser, whom they'd spoken to that could help raise funds, and the arrangements with the nursing home that was hosting the performance.

And in those texts and calls, an easygoing companionship had developed between them which was established by spur-of-the-moment remarks and mutual laughter, peppered by recurring, relaxed silences.

She arranged a napkin on her lap. "So what was your urgent need to see me on this sunshiny morning?"

"Well, the first urgent need was that I was hungry. Starved, actually, but not only for food."

Pointedly, she ignored his innuendo, as well as the flush of heat creeping up her cheeks. Self-consciously, she tucked a strand of hair behind her ear.

Earlier that morning, she'd taken particular care with her appearance, applying rosy lip gloss. Then she'd brushed her black hair until it gleamed and refrained from wearing her usual woolen beanie.

"Well, I'm starved for conversation," she joked.

"I told you about myself." He dove into his croissant. "Now I'd like to learn more about you."

"We've corresponded nearly every day since we met."

"And from the little I gathered from your brief responses, you were adopted from South Korea when you were six months old." He reached for his coffee cup. "Is Holly the name you were born with?"

"I didn't have a name. I was dropped off on a church's stairs."

He stopped in the middle of drinking his coffee. "Truthfully?"

"Many children in Korea are abandoned. Many more are abandoned all over the world."

His stunned expression prompted Holly to explain, "Nonetheless, I believe I was loved by my birth mother. She chose to give me the advantages of adoption—a healthy home and solid education—opportunities she couldn't have provided as a single parent. Most likely she had limited choices, and she 'abandoned' me in a way that permitted me to be found."

He sent her a blank look. "So, who named you? Your adoptive parents?"

"Yes. I was born four weeks premature and required hospitalization in South Korea, which was why I wasn't adopted immediately. Because my birthday is January first and near Christmas, my parents called me Holly. They were Asian as well."

He put his cup down. "They must have been thrilled with an adorable baby girl to cherish."

"Perhaps in the beginning." She nibbled at her brownie. "But as I grew older, I acted out. I assumed I was the only Asian adoptee in town and felt out of place."

He set down his croissant and regarded her. "Were you?"

"No. There is an extensive Asian community in this area. Still, as a child I was bullied for being homely and awkward."

"Surely not?" He leaned forward and gently cupped her chin. "Looking at you, that's hard to believe."

Airily, she waved him off. "The teenage years are difficult for a girl who hasn't figured out where she belongs. Maybe my insecurity showed."

"You were special. You were chosen by your adoptive parents." His brown eyes reminded her of the finest chocolate, and involuntarily, she memorized them. Oftentimes, the scorching heat of his gaze melted her. Now that gaze was slightly hard, as if he was ready to protect her from the insensitive actualities of the real world.

She repaid his protectiveness with a sincere smile.

"You must have fought off the boys in droves once you hit

high school." He threw a quick, grim laugh, and the thought crossed her mind that he might be jealous.

"I was short and skinny, and no guy even looked cross-eyed at me." She reflected on those distressing, uncomfortable years, knowing she'd been thankful for Charity's friendship. Later on, when they'd reached adulthood, Charity often reminded Holly that God was in everyone's heart, even the classmates who had cruelly tormented her. Often, she spoke about sadness and happiness growing together.

"Praise God when things go perfectly," she'd advised. *"And praise God when they don't."*

"Fast forward, and you could be a model on a runway," Tim was saying.

Though she glowed at the flattery, Holly reverted to their earlier conversation. "Certainly, Snowflake and the surrounding areas are welcoming and diverse. The residents are down-to-earth and genuine."

Tim responded by folding his arms and leaning back. "Tell me about your parents. I spoke honestly about mine over hot chocolate and doughnuts."

She caught the aloofness that threaded his tone whenever he mentioned his mother or father, and perceived the hidden frustration and sadness and, yes, bitterness.

"They were loving and bighearted. Both were missionaries and adopted me later in life." Holly fiddled with the charm bracelet on her wrist, hearkening back to her father's chuckle, her mother's arms enfolding her. The delicate scent of violets and shared giggles and bedtime stories enveloped her.

"You mentioned in one of our phone conversations that they passed away?" he asked.

She took a deep breath. It was a question that was challenging to answer, despite the five years that had gone by. She'd learned a hard lesson the day they died—that the people she loved could be taken away from her in an instant.

Precariously close to tears, she fingered the silver charms. "Their small plane went down on a missions trip in Asia. I was supposed to go, but my work schedule interfered at the last minute."

Soon afterward, she'd met Jim and plunged headfirst into a hasty marriage. With hindsight, she'd figured out that she'd coped with the void in her life, seeking to fill it with love and companionship, and had married a man incapable of either.

Tim's steady fingers covered hers. "I expressed my sympathy the other day, but I'm truly sorry for your loss."

"Thank you. This bracelet was a gift from my mother. She bought all the charms too."

He lifted her wrist and inspected each charm individually as she described the momentous occasions in her life.

"By the way, did I mention that you look as beautiful as your charm bracelet?" His intimate grin, the way he adeptly piloted the conversation in a different direction, prompted her heart to do a little flip in her chest. He lifted her hand and kissed it.

"I remind you of a charm bracelet?" she challenged with a jaunty smile.

"A beautiful one."

She busied herself with stirring her latte and beamed. "Thank you. Again."

Many folks had complimented her beauty once she reached college, a respective number of men poetically expressive. She'd extended a gracious acknowledgement while harboring the belief that they weren't speaking the truth. With clear precision she would flashback to the tongue-tied girl she'd been, the girl who'd worn glasses and been nicknamed a studious geek. And sometimes, even if she didn't entirely admit it to herself, the baby who had been abandoned in South Korea.

While she'd attempted to tuck away those long-ago

memories of youth, as an adult she placed little significance on something as fickle as external prettiness.

"I've learned from God that I'm sufficient just the way I am. I'm sufficiently attractive and sufficiently tall."

Tim grinned. "You're five feet."

"That's tall." She recited a favorite pastor's message that had been her mantra through those difficult adolescent years. "God made me, and He is perfect."

"I'm not following."

"I'm enough because God is in me. My talent and intelligence are sufficient."

Without taking his gaze from her face, Tim replied, "I agree."

"It took me a long time to come to peace with that. And Tim, you're enough too."

"With all my baggage?" Despite his outward unconcern, his voice caught ever so slightly.

She clutched her hands together. "I'm subbing at Snowflake Chapel for Sunday's service. I'll be playing Christmas carols, and you're welcome to attend. You mentioned you like 'Silent Night.'" She kept her tone neutral, but inwardly entertained the wish that he would accept her offer.

"Nope. Not my thing, Holly." Idly, he traced his forefinger along the table's wooden surface. His fingers were rough and callused. He was a man who worked with his hands. This charismatic man sitting across from her wasn't a television star anymore. "Thanks for accepting my invitation to see me today," he added.

Accepting? No decision there.

Anytime, she wanted to blurt. Instead, she viewed his guarded expression, his unswerving approach to navigating their discussion away from church.

They ate in quiet camaraderie, interspersed with Tim's queries regarding Jasmine and her mother.

When they finished, a college-aged woman with spiked blond hair wended past the other tables to them, ready to whisk off their plates. "Dessert?" she suggested, and Holly debated. The excellent service in the shop made her wish they had dined somewhere else. Her time with Tim had gone by much too fast. They'd been in the coffee shop less than an hour.

"No dessert for me," Tim told the waitress, grinning at Holly's quirked eyebrow.

"I thought you said—"

"Seeing you is a heap full of sweetness for a Saturday morning, and enough for any man."

Holly rolled her eyes. "Uh-huh. Me and your three packets of sugar."

With a smirk, the waitress placed the check between them.

Neatly, Tim covered the bill with his hand before Holly tugged it toward her.

"My treat, remember?" He reached into his pocket and laid several bills on the table. "No change," he instructed the waitress.

"Thanks, Tim. Annie's cooking in the kitchen but saw you come in. She said hello." Friendly and breezy, the waitress swept up the bills and carried their plates away.

"Who is Annie?" Holly asked. Through the large glass window, she watched pedestrians with ruddy cheeks hurrying along the sidewalk.

"The owner of the place."

"And the waitress knows your first name?"

"I've lived in Colorado ever since I was born, except for my stint in California." He gave an unabashed smile. "When I was a child, I came here with my grandfather."

"Where was your mother? Was she with your grandmother?"

"Sometimes. Other times, she'd take off for a spell and leave me with my grandparents. We never quite knew when she'd come back."

Or if.

She expected him to say more.

How long did his mother leave him? Days? Weeks? Months? Unnerved, Holly waited while a hush took up the space between them.

"Tim?" she eventually said.

"Did you want to ask anything else?" He looked at her as if he'd practically forgotten she sat across from him.

"Not unless you want to tell me more about yourself and—"

"Let's move on to your fund-raising business, all right?" It wasn't a question. The discussion concerning his mother was clearly over.

Holly didn't think she could ever learn enough about him to be satisfied, but she understood that his feelings about his past needed to be respected.

"Yes, of course." She picked up her latte and gazed at him over the cup, attempting to banish the downhearted mood that had settled. "Is Ralph making progress on the shelter?"

"He began the initial-stage fix, which is installing cables and wiring." Tim slid his coffee cup to the side of the table. "His crew removed furniture and carpeting and are running wires under the floorboards, through the walls and in the ceiling. New back boxes have been fitted, and sockets and switches are being rewired."

"The shelter needs all that?"

"Present-day demands are different from the past. High-tech is a part of everyday life, so might as well do it now when they're rewiring."

"So that's just the first stage?" She shook her head. "There's a considerable amount of work involved."

"Ralph and Lou are using a graph, so they're literally on the same page."

"What's the second stage?"

"The floor, ceiling, and walls are replastered, modern light fittings, switch plates, you name it."

"How is the timeline?"

"So far, Ralph and his crew are on track." When she reached for her cup, Tim lightly touched her arm. "Holly, your contribution is an immense help. You came at exactly the right time."

"God's timing is perfect, and every moment matters." She quoted another beloved saying from her pastor.

"Every moment matters," Tim repeated with a wide smile. "I like that. So let's make the most of it by spending the afternoon together."

"Don't you have to work?"

"Not on Saturday." Boyishly, he grinned. "And you aren't teaching any lessons, so you're free."

She swallowed a last gulp of latte. "Are you certain you know my schedule?"

"I memorized your texts, remember?"

She couldn't help her smile. He seemed to regard their texts as a higher form of communication, to be studied, analyzed, and gauged. "Tim, I may not be teaching, but I arranged to stop by the nursing home to prepare the final recital arrangements. Consequently, I'm not free."

"You're an educator, correct?"

"Yes."

"Educators are fond of learning new skills, right?"

She eyed him warily. "What did you have in mind?"

"The nursing home is right down the street from the ice-skating rink."

"So?"

"So, Miss Kim, we can visit the nursing home first and spend time with the residents." He grinned, extending his hand and bringing her to her feet. "Afterward, I'll teach you how to ice skate. And I'm looking forward to your reaction when you see the neon sign that Ralph installed."

CHAPTER NINE

$\mathcal{F}$our days later, Tim was still grinning when he parked his truck near town and walked the short distance to Musical Notes, the local music store.

Flurries were blanketing Snowflake in a fresh covering as evening neared. It was as if he'd phased into a scene from Norman Rockwell's colorful oil painting, *Main Street At Christmas*, complete with the faded brick town hall and country store. All Snowflake lacked were the vintage automobiles.

Sprigs of mistletoe and holly intermingled with whiffs of pine, and candlelight spilled across the pathways.

Taking Holly ice-skating had been a splendid idea, he decided as he neared the store. The rink had been a cacophony of giggling children and adults, and the bustle of hockey and figure skaters competing for ice time reminded him of his limited seasons as a high school hockey player.

Despite having never ice-skated before, she'd been a good sport.

She was infinitely appealing—her dark almond-shaped eyes and black hair flying with abandon over her shoulders—

and she possessed an elegant poise when she'd eventually skated around the rink twice without falling.

Her movements had been graceful, the gentle sway of her hips alluring.

"I did it!" she exclaimed as she skated back to him, her pert nose held high, her fine, sculpted cheekbones flushed with excitement.

Wholeheartedly, he'd applauded.

Because, why not? She was stunning.

He'd been attracted to her since the first night they'd met at the shelter. He recalled her stunned stare when he'd asked if she was homeless and needed a room.

In the ensuing days, she'd occupied all his attention. Brilliant and gifted, righteous and honorable, all wrapped up into one mesmerizing package.

He'd missed seeing her, understanding that she was entrenched in organizing the final fund-raising details and juggling a demanding full-time teaching schedule. Still, he had texted her numerous times each day and phoned her in the evening.

And now he wanted to buy her a gift. Nothing elaborate, just a thank you for all she'd accomplished, and the happiness she'd given him.

In jovial spirits, he brushed a fluffy snowflake off his face and couldn't contain the expanded emotions in his chest. He was behaving like an infatuated adolescent boy.

His mind went back to their day together. After they'd ice-skated, Holly had requested that he build a snowman with her. With her hair tucked beneath a forest-green beanie and her clear complexion devoid of makeup, she was magnificent, and thoughts about anything other than her vanished.

"Sure," he replied, although he never remembered ever actually building a snowman before.

Because again, why not?

And then she did the most childish thing as they strolled toward Cedar Lane Park. She stuck out her foot and tripped him, and he fell into a pile of snow like a piece of sawed timber.

As he lay sprawled on the ground, he'd gaped up at her cherubic grin. "What was that for?"

"Let's call it payback for teaching me how to ice-skate while the entire town of Snowflake watched me fall a half-dozen times."

"But what about when you got up? Do those times count?" He brushed snow from his jacket and advanced on her as if he were a silent leopard ready to pounce.

"Don't you dare, Tim." Stifling a giggle, she backed away.

He made a grab for her, she twisted, and he tumbled forward into another high snowdrift.

Hands primly on her hips, she hovered over him. As ever, her eyes held him spellbound, an intense dark brown, thickly fringed by long lashes. Eyes that were pure and tender.

However, as he was quickly understanding, the true glimpse of the woman was her determined chin and alert gaze.

"Are you lounging there all afternoon?" She rocked on her heels and tossed her hair back, and all he craved was to gather her in his arms and kiss her full lips.

Instead, he fixated on the trees standing starkly above him and the dove-gray sky covered in clouds. "It depends on whether you'll try to push me down again."

"I didn't push you. I tripped you, and it was bad of me." Her gaze sparkled with mischief. "Are you hurt?"

"Only my pride." He gave a guileless smile and held out his hand. "Will you help me up?"

Exactly as he figured she would, she extended her hand, and he pulled her down beside him. With a shriek of merriment, she paused to catch her breath as he curved her onto her back.

"That's the thanks I get for teaching you how to ice-skate?" he challenged.

She giggled and squirmed. "Yes."

"Say thank you."

His answer was a face full of snow while she giggled louder.

"Now I deserve a thank you *and* an apology." He mopped the snow from his face, but when she started to scramble to her feet, he linked his arms around her waist.

"I didn't hear you," he whispered in her ear.

"I'm sorry." Out of breath with laughter, she gasped, "And thank you."

"A vast improvement." He nuzzled her nape. "Kiss me and we'll make up." His lips slanted over hers, and he tightened his hold. With a quiet sigh, she molded herself to him. "Holly, you are so beautiful," he murmured.

And the thought came. If only they could stay like this.

She was with him, he could see her, feel her enticing lips on his.

But then snowflakes began to fall, swirling in all directions, and he feared he would lose her in the thickening flurries. Just as he'd feared losing everyone he loved—his mother, his father, his grandparents. And he had, for they were gone.

He cautioned himself that this was present day and here was Holly. She was honest and vital and kissing him back in delightful surrender. Their future was unexplored, their pasts filled with obstacles, but with her he felt entirely at peace and in agreement with a world that hadn't lived up to his expectations.

That is, not until now.

A few minutes later, the snow stopped, and the clouds cleared. He helped her to her feet and reached for her hand—

two people falling in love, strolling outdoors beneath the dazzling vastness of a winter sky, holding hands. They were surrounded by a Jack Frost wonderland.

He squeezed her gloved fingers. Her hand fit into his as if she were made for him.

And there was no mistaking his feelings, because he was in love with her.

She was free of the pretensions he'd witnessed in Hollywood. She was funny and enthralling and generous. And she was bursting with affection for her students, most notably Jasmine.

Her love for God was forever present, and she clearly accepted God's gift of salvation. "Faith and love begins on the inside," she'd declared, and he was humbled by her attributes, particularly kindness.

Once they arrived at the park, they located a flat, shady area near the gazebo. Nearby on Snow Hill, a popular hilltop ideal for sledding and inner tubing, children zipped down and landed at the bottom. Their parents watched, cheered and hastened down the hill.

"Tim?" Holly said as she shaped and flattened the top of a medium sized snowball.

Whenever she spoke his name, the melodic sound of her voice had a hypnotizing effect on him.

"Hmm?" He evened out the edges of a gigantic snowball and fixed it on the ground. To his astonished pleasure, she made a great show of liking his creation, though he'd only just started. But then, as he'd discovered, she had an ability for making even the ordinary seem extraordinary.

"We've been acquainted only a short while, yet it seems like we've been friends forever," she said. "We shared a great deal about ourselves."

"I've revealed more to you than anyone. We're certainly

never at a loss for words." He paused, observing her. "I like to think we're more than friends."

She polished the angles of the snowball she'd placed on top of his, then gazed up at him. "I would too," she said quietly.

He heard the uncertainty in her voice and his breath halted. Unreservedly and effectively, she was beginning to thaw his heart.

Briefly, he closed his eyes, pondering why she had this magical effect on him. A few seconds later, he managed to speak. "How does the phrase, *a couple,* sound?"

He was surprised at how effortlessly the words came. He'd avoided serious relationships with women and any endearments he'd used were surface only.

"I like it," Holly was saying. "We're a couple, then."

"Let's shake on it." He extended his hand. "Deal?"

She laughed and shook. "Deal."

He lifted her into his arms, twirled her around, and thoroughly kissed her.

As he held her, he reflected on her biggest surprise, which had occurred when they'd parked in front of the ice-skating rink.

Tim had hurried around his truck to open the door for her, looking forward to her reaction when she saw the neon sign Ralph had fixed to the entrance of the rink.

Lips parted, she stared, while he suppressed a chuckle.

"Every moment matters." She enunciated the words she read in a shaky tone, then veered to him. "The owners of this rink must attend my church. They obviously chose this phrase after they heard the pastor's sermon."

"Could be," he said with mild cynicism. "I'd wondered where they got that slogan, and then when you said the same thing in the coffee shop ..."

"*Every moment matters* is more than a slogan, Tim." Their

gazes held. "It's a way of life whether you attend church or not."

Their silence was charged with a growing, mounting awareness for each other. He felt it, because there was no denying its existence; and by the softening of her expression, Holly felt it too.

Now, Tim rehearsed exactly what he'd say to her when next they were together. He wanted them to spend Christmas together. He didn't usually celebrate the holiday, save for serving meals in a Denver soup kitchen in the morning. He didn't cook, so he'd usually bring leftovers back to his apartment, or order a takeout pizza and spend Christmas afternoon reading by himself.

Of course Felicia, his ex-girlfriend, would observe the holiday in high style. Fortunately, that high style didn't include him, and there was no wandering through that mine field anymore of struggling to satisfy her with lavish dinners at overpriced restaurants.

He'd broken things off with her shortly after he'd met Holly. It had been insanity to get involved with Felicia in the first place, but he knew she cared for him.

The breakup had been quick and honest. He saw her in person and tried to do everything right.

She'd been angry. She'd screamed at him. And then it was over.

At the intersection of Main Street, Tim crossed at the stoplight. Outside the entrance to Musical Notes, he paused and rubbed the back of his neck. He hadn't purchased a gift in years, and then only once, when he was twelve and waiting for his mother's recent disappearance to end. Had she been in a treatment program, or run off hot-rodding with her latest boyfriend? He couldn't remember.

It had been mid-December, and the weatherman forecasted a massive storm producing significant snowfall. He'd tried not to upset his grandparents by asking where his mother had gone and spent the empty hours staring out their front bay window at the whirling snowstorm.

He'd watched. He'd waited.

"She'll come back," he'd determinedly told his grandmother. Why wouldn't she? He was an exemplary son, a son to be proud of, so of course his mother wouldn't leave him.

Two days later, Ralph, who worked with his grandfather on construction jobs, had taken Tim shopping. He'd earned a few dollars by running errands for his grandfather at the construction sites.

That day, he'd bought his mother a Christmas gift.

Tim shook his head, chiding himself for overthinking.

This wasn't the same. He wasn't buying a Christmas gift for Holly. He was buying a thank-you gift because of her generous contribution to the community.

And because they were ... a couple.

Besides, his mother and Holly were entirely different people.

He pushed the door to the shop wide open and banished the old memories.

The timbered space was crammed with musically themed gifts, from pencil pouches to statues of composers, to frames embellished with string instruments and posters of Beethoven and Bach.

"Do you sell charms for a bracelet?" he asked the middle-aged salesclerk behind the counter, rushing his words. Thoroughly engrossed in scrolling through her cell phone, she gave a start and swiveled around.

"Yes." She beamed. "And anything musical you can imagine."

Tim took a step forward. "I'd like to purchase a charm."

"Brilliant." She ushered him to a display stand. "Any particular instrument?"

"She plays piano, but she already has a piano charm." He picked through the charms, examining each one.

"Gold or silver?"

"Silver. But she wants to learn how to play the accordion." He perused the display and selected a sterling silver accordion charm polished to a shiny finish.

"This charm is accordion accurate," the sales clerk said.

"Music isn't my forte." He chuckled a little too loudly at his pun. His insecurity about purchasing a gift for someone was showing.

Suppose Holly didn't like it? Or worse, suppose she discarded his gift in search of something more appealing, as his mother had done?

"See?" The clerk rode her thumb across the accordion's tiny keyboard. "Complete with white and black keys similar to a piano."

He nodded. "I'll take it."

"Our store offers gift wrapping at no extra charge."

"Sure." He'd only wrapped one gift in his life, a young boy's clumsy attempts using the Sunday newspaper comics and string.

"Hello, Mr. Inspector! I mean, Mr. Stewart."

A chirpy young voice prompted Tim to spin around. "Jasmine, what are you doing here? And please, call me Mr. Tim."

Jasmine, carrying an armful of music, sprinted to him. "Okay."

"What are you doing here?" he repeated.

"I just finished practicing in the back room. Miss Kim and I are playing 'Silent Night.' It's a duet arrangement."

He grinned. "So I heard."

"And I counted the beats out loud for each measure so I don't go faster than Miss Kim." Perky-pink flags of color enhanced Jasmine's pale cheeks. "I'm preparing a solo too. 'We Three Kings of Orient Are.' Have you ever heard it?"

"Yes. Many times." He paid for the package, carefully

wrapped in ivory paper embellished with lime-green musical notes, and he placed it in a purple bag embossed with the store's logo.

His gaze strayed. "Where's your mother?"

"Working." Jasmine scooped up a heavy quilted coat from a peg rack and traded her shoes for a pair of glittery shearling boots. "Mr. Tim, guess what else?"

"What else?"

The slight girl fairly beamed with excitement. "I won't need to practice at the music store anymore because I'm going to live with Miss Kim. She's been alone since her divorce, so I'll keep her company."

He froze, nearly gasping while his brain recorded disbelief. *Holly had been married?* Never once had she mentioned it.

And what was this about Jasmine living with her?

"Is that what she said?" he casually asked.

"Yep. It's all arranged."

"How?" He struggled to assimilate everything. "Miss Kim lives in Pine Cone Valley."

"I know. I went to her house every week for piano lessons."

"When?" He heard his voice. He'd raised it. "When are you moving in with her?"

"This afternoon."

"With your ... mother?"

"No." Jasmine filed her music into a canvas bag and hoisted it over her shoulder. The strap slipped off, and she slid it back up her arm. "My mother isn't coming."

Then how ...

Unable to extend any more than a head bob, he kept his features bland.

Once he exited the store, the questions exploded in his mind.

Had Jasmine's mother relapsed? Was that why Jasmine

was staying with Holly? Or was Holly planning to take over the little girl's life?

His muscles quivered and his body tensed.

Memories of the incidents when the "men in suits," as his mother had called them, threatened to remove Tim from her home, or rather, lack of home, whenever she lost the battle to her addictions, climbed to the surface.

No. It couldn't be. That wasn't Holly. She'd never take Jasmine away from her mother. She loved the girl and wanted what was best for her. And a child belonged with a loving, caring parent. Holly knew that. Everyone knew that.

His heart hollered the denial. But his mind mulled over Holly's words, the smidgens of conversations regarding Jasmine, and his pulse raced.

"I would do anything for that little girl."

CHAPTER TEN

$\mathcal{S}$eated on the tufted couch in her living room, a pen in hand and a mountain of paper beside her, Holly studied her list of things left to do. The baby grand piano in the nursing home had been tuned, a donation box set up, and her students were prepared. The media had publicized the fund-raiser on television, radio and newspaper at no charge, and colorful brochures noting the date and time were posted in shop windows everywhere.

Plus, an extensive three-part email marketing event had begun, with an announcement sent to area businesses. The first was a Save the Date; the second, an Event Reminder; and the third, a Last Chance email.

The Astra Project Fund-raiser to benefit the Snowflake Homeless Shelter

Holiday Piano Recital at Golden Birch Manor
5 Cedar Lane, Snowflake, Colorado
December 23rd at three o'clock
Bring an ornament for the residents' tree!
Donations accepted at the door

Tim had mentioned that he'd provide the tree, and Holly counted on him staying true to his word.

Luckily, she'd started her annual winter recess, which meant lessons were scheduled only for students who opted to participate in the fund-raiser.

But she hadn't finished decorating her apartment, nor hoisted her "Charlie Brown" tree from the attic.

And she hadn't heard from Tim.

Her hands fluttered, and she set the pen aside. She sagged against the couch, trying to ignore the prick of anguish that came with a stark realization. Tim was avoiding her. He hadn't reached out in days, and her texts had been greeted with replies so short and clipped that she'd actually flinched.

Why had he suddenly lost interest in her?

All the jubilant expectation of spending the holidays with him had drained out of her. And that awareness left her shocked and rejected.

Unfocused, she stared vacantly at the paper.

She'd done it again. She'd placed her trust in a man. A man who obviously considered her nothing more than a diversion that had run its course.

Her chin quivered as she succumbed to a rush of tears. These days, she did that a lot. When at last her tears subsided, she dried her eyes and went in search of a soft cloth to press over them.

That morning, her views had swung the opposite way, and her battered pride had prompted her to push her shoulders back and silently banish him.

Of all the nerve. Of all the insensitive nerve.

She'd thwarted her heartache by telling herself that there was no reason for her sadness. He'd go on to solid-gold charm another woman and ... And so what?

So what if that thought caused her to feel hollow inside?

She rubbed her temples and swung her legs to the side of

the couch, weary of the mental conflict harboring her disbelief and bewilderment.

Finally, she'd decided not to contact him anymore. No longer did she leave him cheery voice mails, or any voice mails at all.

"*How does the phrase* a couple *sound?*" he'd asked.

She'd detected the revealing huskiness in his voice and believed his admission sincere. Apparently the actor could carry off a deliberate deception without a second thought.

Determined that the recital would be a success, she'd resolved that nothing, not even a shattered heart, would preclude her from achieving her goal. Her aunt had pegged Holly's quest as a personal penchant, a private pursuit to raise all the money the shelter needed. And that was exactly what she intended to do.

Nevertheless, she also had an eleven-year-old girl living in her apartment. A girl who left scuff marks on the tiled floor in the foyer and often seemed despondent. A precocious child who chatted only when she was in the mood, Jasmine spent hours after school practicing the piano in Holly's living room, or straggling her legs out in front of her as she flopped on the couch. Hands jammed into jean pockets, she resembled a tiny pixie with round, impish eyes as she declared how bored she was.

Holly suggested she read a book or play with the cat. That occupied the girl for about ten minutes.

The previous afternoon, the principal of the elementary school had phoned because of a discipline issue. Jasmine, it seemed, had a tendency to associate with the wrong crowd, claiming that she should stick with "kids who understood her best."

Considering her age and how she'd been displaced and lived in multiple homes, the principal assured Holly that Jasmine's behavior was normal, and her scores on intelligence tests rated higher than average. Still, Holly spent numerous hours on the phone with Jasmine's mother discussing the situation.

The last morning before winter break, Holly phoned her aunt while Jasmine was in school.

"Try to relate to the depth of Jasmine's plight," Aunt Clementine advised. "Understandably, she misses her mother. Focus on the good news. She secured an excellent job with a generous salary and benefits, and they'll be reunited soon. But I'll continue to pray for them, of course."

Silence surged for a beat.

Holly tapped her foot on the floor. To split the stillness, she inquired, "Are you still seeing Justin, Aunt Clementine?"

"His arm is looped around my shoulders as we speak."

"You both fit in the recliner?" Holly teased with a delicate chuckle.

"We're a perfect match."

Holly smiled at the mental image of two seniors ultimately finding love. "Are you housing any new rescue dogs?" she asked.

As if on cue, a dog bayed.

"One adorable long-eared beagle, and a Yorkshire terrier who insists on yapping at everything."

Holly giggled and then immediately sobered when her aunt inquired, "What's new with Tim?"

She tightened her grip on the cell phone. "I ... I wouldn't know."

"I understood that you texted or saw each other every day." Holly heard a smooch and assumed Justin had kissed her aunt.

"Tim isn't talking to me," Holly replied.

"Why not? What's the problem?"

It was useless to hide the facts. Her aunt was extremely discerning.

"The problem is he's avoided me ever since ..." Frowning, Holly sat up straight as a notion struck her. "Ever since Jasmine moved in. I assumed he liked children. Apparently not."

"So he's aware of the situation with Jasmine?"

"Yes. She met him in the music store in Snowflake and told him before I had the chance." Holly gulped to steady her emotions. "It all happened so quickly when her mother was hired for her dream job in Denver."

"And now along with caring for a youngster, your fund-raiser is in a couple days," Aunt Clementine said.

"Tim is supposed to donate the tree. I hope he will."

"If he said he will, then I have no doubt he will. He seems a man of his word, so I wouldn't worry. Have faith."

"I do."

"Then the odds are in your favor. Tim will come through."

Holly collapsed against the back of the couch. "Will he?"

"Your expectations flow from God. In the end, it is God who provides."

Holly gained strength from her aunt's belief, as well as her conviction regarding Tim's solid character.

"I invited him to the recital so often that I lost count, but his replies were always noncommittal."

"What did he say exactly?" her aunt asked.

"Just something about working that day." Holly bit her lower lip. "But the town offices are closed for the holiday break, so he wouldn't work unless he was on call."

"From the sounds of your romance, I presumed you were falling in love."

"You were wrong." Unconsciously, Holly pressed a hand to her heart. "We only met a short while ago."

"But still, it sounded wonderful."

But still, it WAS wonderful.

So wonderful, in fact, that when Holly clicked off, she curled her arms across her chest and wept.

*F*orty-eight hours later, Holly entered the lobby of the Golden Birch nursing home, carefully balancing a pile of music with a container of Chinese Christmas cookies stacked on top. Garland outlined the door, spelling out the words *Noel* and *Joy*.

She'd chosen to wear cashmere slacks in a rosebud-pink, and a notch-collared faux wrap blouse in a vibrant silk print. She'd arranged her hair into an elegant chignon at her nape, secured with a faux diamond clip, and a pair of tiny diamond earrings. Her gingerbread-colored tote bag doubled as a handbag.

Jasmine, endearing in a red ruffled lace dress and black patent leather shoes, her blond hair styled in ringlets, skipped beside Holly. Clutching her music to her thin chest, she glowed with optimism when her mother hugged her.

As arranged, Emily had met them at the recital and would take Jasmine home with her to Denver when it was over.

"Thank you, Holly, for allowing Jasmine to finish the semester in Snowflake while I started my new job," Emily said. "It was helpful that you drove her to and from school every day."

"No worries," Holly said. "Jasmine even helped me set the table for dinner two nights in a row. That is, when she didn't practice or play with my cat."

Holly realized that Jasmine's mother deserved whole-hearted accolades. She was a single parent who'd resolved to make a better life for her and her daughter and raising a child certainly wasn't easy. "I'm happy this is all working out for you."

The previous afternoon after church service at Snowflake

Chapel, Holly and Jasmine had baked Christmas cookies. They'd snacked on leftover butterscotch chips and velvety chocolate that melted on their tongues, and Holly had explained that the Chinese Christmas cookie recipe was from Tina, her college friend.

And they'd discussed Pastor Tom's sermon based on John 3:16, concerning God's unconditional love. "The outlook in your heart replicates the judgments in your mind," he'd preached. "God sees how your narrative begins and ends. He loves us, even though we oftentimes feel inadequate and make mistakes."

Holly had taken the message to heart and prayed for forgiveness. She'd recognized that she'd lost patience with Jasmine on occasion.

She was brought back to the present when she shifted to allow a professional caregiver to pass. He wheeled a white-haired fellow in a wheelchair and both extended a smile. Inspired, she smiled back. The home was evidently devoted to its seniors.

To celebrate the holiday, multicolored lights in the shape of an angel were affixed with tape to a blank wall, and individual stockings were tacked on each resident's door. Down the hall, an engaging game of bingo sounded over a loudspeaker, and an outdoor area beyond the dining room enabled residents to enjoy the gardens when the weather was warm.

While parents made space for the residents, Holly's students guided the elderly men and women, some with canes, others with walkers, to the enormous parlor where the recital would take place. The glossy ebony-black piano commanded center stage.

In the meantime, Holly conferred with the director about organizing the refreshments and donation box, and reminded the attendees to hang their ornament on the eight-foot-tall tree.

"The crowd is larger than we expected and donations started pouring in yesterday," the director informed Holly. Her ash-blond hair was coiled in an upsweep, a bouffant hair-style that Holly hadn't seen in years. She headed toward the hallway and began setting up extra chairs.

"Yes, I'm thrilled." Holly tailed her. "Thank you for allowing us to perform."

"Our pleasure. And the tree." The director regarded the tall pine. "The tree was donated by Mr. Timothy Stewart. A local Christmas tree farm delivered it this morning."

"Is he here?" Holly couldn't help herself, her anxious gaze pinned to the front door. Then she foolishly regarded the tree, as if Tim might materialize from behind it. "The man who arranged the delivery?"

"He was here earlier, but disappeared shortly before you arrived."

Holly stopped herself from asking any more questions about him. "Right. Thanks." She reverted to her professional teacher tone and stepped into the parlor.

A half hour before the recital, Holly knelt by each of her thirty students, who ranged in age from six to eighteen years old. She offered encouragement and reminded them to sing along with the Christmas hymns for the finale. However, she was no match for their eagerness, their love of music, which, she ascertained with a tinge of pride, she'd helped to instill in them.

At five minutes before the hour, Holly's heart rate doubled in nervous anticipation. She seated herself in the front row and creased the page turn of the first piece, "Silent Night." She'd decided to commence with a strong opening, foreseeing a seamless performance because she and Jasmine had practiced the duet for hours.

"You don't like Silent Night?" she'd asked Tim.

"Everyone likes Silent Night," he'd replied.

Her eyes burned with tears. A lump settled in her throat, and she swallowed determinedly. She certainly couldn't break down here. She was a woman with mettle and resolve.

Something caused her to swivel, and her stomach fluttered. Privately, she wished that a broad-shouldered handsome man had shown up at the last minute to support her and her cause. Instead, she locked gazes with a recognizable fellow sporting a plaid coat and thick eyeglasses. He'd planted himself at the far end of the parlor and passed her a sociable nod.

"Ralph?" She chewed on her trembling lip and prayed her disappointment didn't show. She came to her feet and hastened to him. "What are you doing here?"

"I finished work early, and I'm always up for supporting a good cause." He gave a half-laugh. "After the recital, let's meet in town at The Little Corner Bistro. Say, seven o'clock? They close at eight."

It was a subtle order, not a request.

"All right."

"Will you be bringing Jasmine?" he asked.

Startled, she shuffled back. "No. She'll be with her mother."

"Excellent. That's where a child belongs." He stepped away. "Be prompt. I have some news you'll want to hear."

CHAPTER ELEVEN

They'd done it. The recital was over. By the ringing applause from the residents, friends, and family, the students' performances and sing-along were an emphatic success. Even better, they'd raised an additional five hundred dollars, and the director assured Holly that donations would continue throughout the holiday season.

Holly kissed Jasmine and her mother good-bye, and congratulated the girl on a flawless recital. She promised to send recommendations for piano teachers in the Denver area. On their way out, Holly overheard Emily reveal to Jasmine that they were heading to the humane society. A seven-year-old shih tzu named Leo had been given up for adoption because the owner's landlord didn't allow pets.

"But our new landlord does?" Jasmine asked tentatively.

"Yes. He gave the okay. Merry Christmas, Jasmine!"

The girl flung her arms around her mother's neck. "Merry Christmas, Mommy!"

After lemonade was served and the remaining students and parents departed, Holly lingered to converse with the residents and joined in a high-spirited game of bingo.

At six o'clock, she yanked on her coat and headed for the exit. An hour was enough time to drive the short distance to The Little Corner Bistro in town.

"Holly?"

She swiveled at the recognizable male voice, deep and achingly familiar.

Tim perched on the edge of a folding chair, arms crossed, the color rising in his handsome, tanned face. She struggled to still the traitorous responses unfurling within her, struggled to keep her expression blank in the same way he had mastered.

"Excellent recital." He stood and came forward. "You were magnificent."

Guardedly, Holly contemplated him. "How would you know?"

He brushed his hand along her cheek. "I was here."

"I didn't see you." She'd scanned the parlor countless times.

"Do you think I'm lying?"

"I'm not certain what to think anymore when it comes to you."

He reached out to take her hands.

She jerked aside and spun for the door. The director at the front desk peeked up, and Holly ignored her soft bark of laughter.

"She's watching us," Tim murmured. He'd beaten Holly to the door. He propped his hand on the frame, successfully delaying her departure.

Holly sent a commendable imitation of a smile toward the director, committing to revisit on Christmas Eve at three o'clock, which would allow ample time to attend the church service at six. She'd made arrangements to play carols for the residents.

She placed her fingers on the door's brass handle. "Even more of a reason to let me pass, then," she sputtered.

His jaw hardened. "Where's Jasmine?"

"She left already."

"I'll walk you to your car." His tone was as unmoving as his stance. "I ... I bought you a gift."

Her breath caught as she stared up at his earnest, attractive face, and once again she cautioned herself that he'd been a successful actor. "I'm not interested in your gifts. Please excuse me." She wrenched the door open and held a stiff posture as she marched past him.

The nursing home's parking lot was silent and nearly empty. A nipping, icy sleet had begun to fall, fierce and relentless.

Across the street, the neon sign of the ice-skating rink flashed *Every Moment Matters*.

She thrust her freezing hands into her coat pockets and observed the nursing home. Frost clung to the windows and night had fallen. In December, the days grew short so rapidly.

She hurried to her Jeep.

Tim quickened to keep up with her. "Why are you ignoring me?"

Holly grabbed her beanie from her tote bag and drew it over her raw ears. "Now there's a million-dollar question."

"What's that supposed to mean?"

"You're the person who disappeared."

His forehead creased into a scowl. "I've been around the nursing home all day."

"Where? Invisibly?"

"I stayed in the hallway for the entire recital, and rushed out the minute it was finished because I was called to a job in town. I assumed you'd chat a while with your students. I intended to return within a couple hours, and I did." He grasped her forearms. "So, can we talk?"

Meticulously, she wrenched free from his grasp, first one arm, then the other. "No. Not anymore."

"Can I give you ... this?" Undeterred, he smiled, but the smile wavered. "I thought you might like a little something."

She drew a trembling inhale at the sight of the miniature box wrapped in ivory paper, embellished with lime-green musical notes. "Why?" Rubbing a hand over her heart, she readied to end the conversation. Being near him hurt too much.

His smile faded, his eyes bottomless pools of anguish. "Don't you like gifts?" His voice sounded very odd, very unsure.

"Not your gifts, Tim. Please keep it."

With a proud tilt of her head, she whirled, striding away on legs that felt too weak to support her body.

CHAPTER TWELVE

A hollow numbness settled over Holly as she drove the few blocks to The Little Corner Bistro. Instead of being emboldened by refusing Tim, she was despondent, and heavy with remorse for her inexcusably bad behavior.

Negotiating the busy traffic into the center of town took longer than she anticipated, compounded by waiting at an intersection until there was a break. Nonetheless, she reached the bistro before seven o'clock and parked at the curb. The street was dark save for the bistro's muted pendant lighting stretching from the rustic interior.

As she got out of the car, she hardly noticed the sting of icy pellets on her heated cheeks. Unblinking, she shivered and clutched her coat closer, half hoping that Tim had pursued her. He hadn't, and she shook her head in mock derision, feeling foolish for thinking otherwise.

She shuffled to the front entrance. An illuminated reindeer in the lobby greeted her, along with background instrumental music, a classical rendition of "Silver Bells." White pine roping adorned the mantel of a crackling fireplace, and each tabletop sported a mason jar chock-full of red and green ornaments.

Ralph sat at a table near the back. He sprang to his feet, took her coat and hung it on a coat rack.

"Where's Tim?" He asked so casually that Holly was immediately put on her guard.

"I have no idea." She tugged off her wool beanie and flattened back the wet hair plastered to her cheeks. They both slid into chairs across from each other at the table. "Why?"

"I expected he was coming with you." Ralph's gray eyebrows rose at what he evidently assumed was an oversight. "Didn't you see him after the recital?"

"Only for a short while." Somehow, she kept her tone nonchalant.

A waitress scurried over, gripping a pad to take their orders.

"Peppermint tea for me," Holly said.

Ralph nodded agreement. "The same."

After tea was served, Ralph silently observed Holly while he stirred in cream and sugar.

"Do you want to discuss what happened at the nursing home and why he's not with you?" he asked.

"And spoil a perfect chat? Let's just say we had a disagreement." Ruefully, she shook her head and fixated on the mason jar between them. "Truthfully, I've thought about him so much, I've run out of words."

Ralph's forehead furrowed. "In my opinion, you two care a great deal about each other. However, I'm not certain who is more stubborn, you or Tim."

His reproof made Holly straighten. "It's Tim. He's impossible. I assumed I understood him, but he's an enigma."

Ralph hunched forward. "He was angry when he found out you had taken Jasmine in."

"First, that was none of his business," Holly said. "Second,

Jasmine's mother secured a job in Denver and asked me to keep Jasmine at my apartment so that Jasmine could finish out the school semester. Of course I was happy to help."

A gleam sparked in Ralph's eyes, partially hidden behind his thick glasses. "Ah, so that explains it."

"I don't understand."

"Tim's mother wasn't the best, but she was fiercely protective." Ralph bent his head and surveyed Holly. "She instilled in him a deep fear of being taken by the authorities, an 'us versus them' philosophy. Because of Tim's previous experience, he probably assumed you intended to pull Jasmine away from her mother for good. He's got deep feelings about subjects of that nature."

"So in his mind he charged me with a crime, and the verdict was guilty?" Holly drew in a small breath. "All without actually speaking to me?"

"And yet he still came around today and forgave you."

She studied her hands. "For a crime I didn't commit."

"Why didn't you explain Jasmine's situation to him?"

"Well, to begin with, he's completely ignored me these past few days. He didn't respond to my texts or phone calls." Holly broke off, unable to put her heartache into a coherent sentence.

"And that hurt you, because you're in love with him," Ralph replied.

"Yes." Her face heated. She'd blurted her admittance too quickly.

She couldn't bear to face Ralph's perceptive smile and averted her gaze, peering out the double-hung windows facing the street. Sleet had frosted the overhang, and the hand-painted stone fountains flanking the entrance were glazed with ice.

"Good news." Ralph didn't hide the delight in his gravelly voice. "He's in love with you too."

Suppressing the flare of optimism in her chest, Holly kept her gaze on the outside fountains. There was nothing else to say, but in all honesty, there was everything.

"Does Tim ignore every woman he loves?" she finally asked.

"To my knowledge, he's never loved another woman. Sure, he dates women and treats them with respect, but he never reveals anything about himself. But you—you touched a nerve. You brought out a part of his past he's tried to suppress." Ralph shook his head. "Instead of confronting you, he closed up. That's what he does."

"Why?" Holly's mouth went dry. "We've spent hours talking about our lives."

"But not talking about everything." Ralph fairly swooped down on her reply. "Tim is a complex man, Holly. I first met him when he was a little boy. He was lovable, appealing, and into mischief at every opportunity despite his attempts to appear angelic."

Holly smiled and leaned forward. "Please tell me more."

"He was smart, sharp as a razor." Ralph grinned. "And solid and sunny. Any mother would be bursting with pride to have him as her son."

"Any mother except ... his?"

"Oh, she was proud, all right. Sometimes. Sometimes not. It all depended on if her addictions got the better of her. Tim never knew where he was going to wake up from one week to the next—under a bridge or at his grandparent's house. His mother was an original and even called herself Astra for a spell. When I saw the name on your advertisements, I knew Tim had told you about her."

"A star of hope," Holly said. "I must have explained the significance of that name a hundred times this week."

"Or a falling star."

"I refuse to believe that." She frowned. "Where did you and Tim meet?"

"His grandfather and I were friends since we were both in the building trade." Ralph lifted his cup to his lips, and Holly noticed a subtle tremor in his hand. "We all called him Timmy back then, that is until he forbade it."

"How old was he at the time?"

"Probably nine."

"And his mother?" This close, Holly counted the numerous lines on Ralph's wide forehead, the gray whisker stubbles on his chin. "From what I gather, she was everything to him, although he shuts down whenever it comes to actually discussing her."

"Despite her lifestyle, she was the center of his life." Ralph folded his hands. "Can I tell you a story?"

"Of course." There was the tiniest catch in her voice. She wondered if Ralph noticed.

"His mother was drop-dead gorgeous until her addictions wore her looks away. One Christmas soon after I met them, she left him with his grandparents, and, after a few days, he begged me to take him shopping. He'd saved some money by working for his grandfather, doing odd jobs at the construction site, and he wanted to buy her some jewelry. He found an adorable charm on clearance that was engraved with the words *Mama Bear*."

"Precious."

"To you. To me." Ralph fell silent for a heartbeat. Firelight cast dim shadows on his creased cheeks. "Tim didn't have the money for the store gift-wrapping, so he wrapped it himself with old newspaper and string."

"His mother must have been thrilled when he gave her the gift."

"I was at his grandparents' when she finally showed up on

Christmas Eve. Tim was so excited he could hardly keep still. He grabbed the gift from beneath the tree and pressed it into her hands. 'Mommy, I got you a gift,' he said. He looked so small standing there." Ralph's tone rang with sadness. "I assumed she would welcome him into her arms and apologize for being gone so long. And that she'd make a big show of opening it."

"Didn't she?"

"No. A car horn, her latest boyfriend, and off she went out the door."

Holly's entire body tensed. She was unable to hide her sadness and righteous anger for the little boy Tim had once been, for the man she loved.

For she had, indeed, fallen in love with him.

"What happened next?" She dabbed tears from the corner of her eyes.

"He called out to her, he still held the gift. She dismissed it. Dismissed him." Ralph's eyes were damp. "Sure, he probably spent exorbitant amounts of money on women when he was in Hollywood, but he never actually bought them a present. He's been blessed in his professional life because of his exceptional looks and hard work ethic. In his personal life, not so blessed."

A painful silence emerged, despite the bustle as the bistro began shutting down for the night. Holly was perilously close to weeping, recalling her heated discussion with Tim only an hour before, and the contemptuous way she'd informed him to keep his gift.

She covered her face with her hands. "Did he ever forgive his mother for her callousness?"

"In one sense, yes, but forgiveness is difficult. Tim's heart is kind, but he's careful. Understandably so. It takes a big person to forgive."

"'As far as the east is from the west, so far has he removed our transgressions from us.'"

"Psalm 103:12," Ralph responded. "I'm a church-going man, and listened closely to Pastor Tom's recent sermon. Does that surprise you?"

Holly smiled at the reference to church. "Not at all. You strike me as a compassionate man, who has obviously formed deep friendships."

"I never married. I wanted to."

Holly chuckled. "Until a few weeks ago, I might have matched you up with my aunt. But now, in her sixties, she is dating a wonderful man."

"I never found the right woman." Ralph held up his left hand, devoid of a wedding band. "Fortunately for Tim, he has."

"I appreciate what you're trying to do, Ralph." With a ragged laugh, Holly reached for her tea. It was cold. "However, your efforts are wasted."

"I read a study once. Within three days, you'll be able to identify whether or not you're attracted to another person."

"Hardly a lifetime. I didn't go to the homeless shelter looking for love."

"Let's call it a fortunate accident then."

"A fortunate accident." She sought to match his upbeat tone. "What's the good news, by the way?"

The waitress pointedly placed a check on the table and peered at her watch, then posted the closed sign on the entrance door.

Ralph paid the bill and got to his feet. "An anonymous businessman in the community has offered to pay the entire rewiring project, and the work should be completed by the end of December. Lou will deposit the money you've given toward services, food, and clothes for the residents."

"Ralph, that's wonderful." He helped Holly on with her coat, and she swung her arms in excitement as they exited. "Who's the businessman?"

He winked. "Anonymous, remember?"

"Is it Tim?"

"I'm not at liberty to tell. But since you mentioned Tim again ... I watched the way he looked at you the night of the tree lighting, and in truth, I was surprised. When he acted in that popular television series, women swarmed all over him. They still do. He's always been immune, which hardly shocks me, given his history. Still, despite the fleeting fame, he's a street kid at heart. Nonetheless, that man is deeply in love with you."

And Holly, in turn, was in love with him.

But would he ever forgive her for being so insensitive—rejecting not only his gift but the man himself?

CHAPTER THIRTEEN

*E*arly on Christmas Eve day, Holly hoisted her spindly tree from her apartment building's attic and arranged it by the living room window. Outside, luminous rays of sun highlighted wintry trees, and a light snowfall resembled crystal lace.

She hadn't heard from Tim, and although the possibility existed, she certainly didn't expect to.

Consequently, she pondered how best to approach him.

Phone? Maybe. Maybe not. Suppose he ignored her calls?

Text? Probably the same.

There was so much she wished to say, so much to explain. But where to begin?

Completely immersed in her musings, she balanced on the garden stool to hang tinsel on the higher branches. From the corner of her eye, she glimpsed the box of ornaments on the floor—the glittering baby-blue icicles, the winter angel, and the lighted manger.

"How does the phrase a couple *sound?"*

Tim's rugged face seared in her mind, and she recalled each detail of their afternoon building a snowman. The scene jerked her from her task, and the restraint she'd relied upon crumpled.

She sank onto her tufted sofa. The tears she'd vowed not to shed streamed down her cheeks.

"I'm sorry, Tim." She wept hot, broken sobs. "How do I ask for your forgiveness? How do I know you won't reject me?"

With a semblance of control, she grabbed her cell phone. Butterscotch skirted across her ankles, purring and flicking his cream-colored tail. She reached down to scratch his head. "I'll stop at the This and That Shop before the nursing home, then I'll return here after the church service," she informed him.

Already dressed in a red crushed-velvet dress that skimmed her curves, Holly styled her hair long and loose. Her silver bracelet decorated her wrist, the charms gaily jingling.

The only thing left was to contact him. Easy. She'd invite him over for Christmas Day. She paused, swallowed and cradled the phone to her chest.

And how would she begin that invitation, exactly? Her courage dissolved as she anticipated his curt reply. Or worse, if he didn't reply at all.

*S*eated in her four-wheel-drive Jeep, Holly focused on the road to the nursing home and arrived at three o'clock. Streetlamps misted beneath a fine snowfall, and the sun struggled to appear through gray clouds.

Earlier, she'd ducked into the This and That Shop to purchase a tree topper. On the spur of the moment, she'd requested the topper be gift wrapped because she planned to give it to a special someone.

Voices were muted as she entered the nursing home. When she walked into the parlor, she noticed quite a few of the residents visited with family members. Holly sat at the piano and introduced herself before launching into the first Christmas carol.

After the sing-along ended, she reminded each man and woman individually how remarkable they were and wished them all a joyous holiday.

After embracing the last resident, she stepped out of the home. Pausing, she hesitated in the parking lot and stared at the unpretentious yet expressive words flashing from the ice-skating rink's neon sign.

Every moment matters.

But it was the person standing beneath the sign who captivated her.

There it was. And there he was.

From his dark furrowed eyebrows to the sturdy jut of his jaw, he was her beloved. The mark of his strong physique, the same potent appeal that had chased her nightly dreams, caused tears to slide down her cheeks.

His hands were at his sides, the familiar cranberry-colored scarf around the neckline of his navy-blue parka.

Silently, he acknowledged her.

The director stepped out from the home, calling to Holly that she had forgotten her music, flapping it in the air. Holly hardly heard her. She rushed through the snow, the parking lot, quicker now, then raced across the street into Tim's outstretched arms.

"What are you doing here?" Her shoulders quaked. Her face nestled against his chest as he embraced her.

"I came for you. I waited." His deep, gripping voice. She'd ached to hear it again. "I wanted to wish you a Merry Christmas. And to tell you I'm sorry. I'm so very sorry."

"I planned to call you, to text." She swallowed the lump of remorse in her throat and curved her arms around him. "I was afraid you'd reject me. There were things I wanted to say, beginning with my apology for the way I treated you yesterday."

"You're forgiven. Now please forgive me." His tone was a raw whisper, hoarse and sincere.

"I forgive you." Her eyes moistened as she gazed intently into his. "You're a good man. You inspire me to become a better person."

"You inspire *me*." He pressed his forefinger to her lips to prevent her from speaking. "To care. Really care, even if I get hurt."

"You won't. I promise." She placed a hand on his chest. Beneath his jacket, his heart beat vital and solid.

He brushed a strand of hair off her cheek. "If I could undo—"

"There's nothing to undo." Her heart constricted with a love so deep that she held him ever closer. "An hour earlier, I felt alone and sad. Now I feel like dancing."

"And singing?" he teased.

"Yes." She sniffed, and a tear trickled down her cheek.

"Then why the tears?"

"Because you're here," she whispered. "And I'm happy."

"Has anyone ever mentioned," he kissed her, leaving her breathless, "that your smile lights up the entire town?"

Her merriment muffled against his chest, before she glanced around at the empty sidewalk. "It's probably wise if we go to my car. I have something for you."

The director still stood on the nursing home's steps, apparently impervious to the cold.

"She isn't going to go inside until she sees us kiss again," Tim murmured.

"Again?" Holly offered a winsome grin. "All this kissing in front of the entire town?"

"Yep." He tightened his hold and lowered his head, and she encouraged his stirring kiss with one of her own.

He was here, Holly thought. On Christmas Eve, Tim was really here.

A half-hour later, evening had fully descended. Tim and Holly were seated in her Jeep, in the parking lot of the nursing home. She sat in the driver's seat, he settled beside her in the passenger seat.

A dozen questions raced through his brain and he drew in a breath.

"I've missed you very, very much," he began.

"I've missed you too."

He responded with a kiss, trailing his fingers through her silky black hair and holding her near. She reacted with the same yearning that had awakened him from sleep and kept him up at night.

"Tim, we need to talk," she said.

"For a while," he granted. But not for long, he grinned.

"When I told you to keep your gift ..." Her features swelled with anguish, her tone subdued. "I was hurt and baffled and lashed out at you."

His grin sobered. "I assumed you were seeking to take Jasmine away from her mother. My judgments were uncalled for."

"Don't ever shut me out like that again. You didn't even allow me a chance to explain."

"I'm sorry." He enfolded her in his arms and kissed the top of her head. "And you were married. You never told me."

She shuddered. "I assumed I would never get over it."

"Did you?"

"Thoroughly. Charity was correct. A joyous tomorrow is straight ahead."

He smiled at her infectious tone. "Because?"

"Because I found you."

"And I found you." He fished in his pocket for the small wrapped gift and presented it to her.

"For Christmas?" she inquired.

"Guess again."

"My birthday?"

"January first is a week away and I'm buying you something special." He would ask her to marry him, to embark on their future together as *a couple*. "This gift is for you for being ... you."

Silently, she unwrapped the package, broke into a wide grin, and leaned forward for a closer look.

"Do you like the charm?" he asked.

"I love it. But how did you remember I wanted to learn how to play the accordion?"

He fastened the charm onto her bracelet and kissed her wrist. "Because, if you recall, I memorized all your texts and our conversations."

"I have something for you too." She reached behind her, then handed him a bag imprinted with the words This and That Shop.

He gazed at the star he unwrapped, a simple five-point design with gold glitter, and smoothed his forefinger along the sleek edges. At one of the most touching moments of his life, he could only smile.

"Thank you," he whispered. His voice was husky and he cleared his throat.

"It's a tree-topper. At first I bought it for myself—for my Christmas tree. But in my heart I knew it was for you."

"Astra," he murmured.

"A shining beacon of hope."

This was Holly's gift. An act of generosity, the true spirit of the holiday, an acceptance of Christian grace and love.

"Will you spend Christmas with me?" she asked. "Will you help me decorate my tree? More often than not, I'm alone."

"So am I."

"I usually order a pizza."

"Me too. Takeout."

Her beautiful face brightened with color, her almond-shaped eyes glistened with love. Tenderly, she touched the tiny accordion charm.

"And I accept," he added. "In fact, I thought you'd never ask." He smiled and peered through the foggy windshield. Arms crossed and a cardigan sweater thrown over her shoulders, the director remained on the nursing home's steps and glared at them. Or was she grinning? He couldn't tell.

"I'm guessing she aims to throw us out of the parking lot," he said.

"Should I tell her I'll pick up my music some other time?"

"You can text her. Tomorrow."

The peal of Snowflake Chapel's church bells made him pause. The first star appeared in the sky, radiant and twinkling.

"Church service begins at six o'clock," Holly said softly.

"I'd like to attend."

He couldn't judge her reaction at first. That is, until she gazed up at him with a radiant smile. "Really?"

"Really."

"God is calling. He must've found you."

"I'm easy to find because I'm with you. If He will take me with all my shortcomings—" Tim wavered. "He's bound to be disappointed."

"You can't disappoint God." She started the car, letting it idle as she hummed "Silent Night." He chuckled. She glanced at him. "You don't like 'Silent Night'?"

"Everyone likes 'Silent Night.'" Laughing quietly, he nuzzled her neck. "And Holly Kim, I love you."

She skimmed her hand against his cheek.

In the midst of a wondrous Christmas Eve, he reflected

on the unexpected circumstances that had brought this exquisite woman into his world.

At the age of thirty-four, when he was toughened by what he'd seen as a child, by what he'd done in Hollywood, he bowed to a consideration he'd never allowed himself.

He was good enough for God. And he was good enough for the woman he cherished.

 HE END

A NOTE FROM JOSIE

Dear Friend,

Thank you for reading *Holly's Gift*, set in the charming fictional town of Snowflake, Colorado.

If you loved this sweet inspirational holiday romance as much as I loved writing it, please help other people find *Holly's Gift* by posting your review.

I've always looked forward to the holiday season, and wanted to give the title, Holly's Gift, personal meaning when Holly offers the hero, Tim, her most precious gift.

A gift of faith.

Like Holly, I am also a pianist, and I happily brought music into the season. Holly's students, notably Jasmine, were an inspiration.

Many of my readers will chuckle about the 7-year-old shih tzu who is adopted in the story, as my shih tzu, Henry, occupies a special corner beside me while I write. He is a sweet dog!

I'd love to meet you in person someday, but in the meantime, all I can offer is a sincere and grateful thank you. Without your support, my books would not be possible.

As I write my next sweet or inspirational romance, remember this: Have you ever tried something you were afraid to try because it mattered so much to you? I did, when I started writing. Take the chance, and just do something you love.

With sincere appreciation,

Josie Riviera

Love sweet romance Christmas stories? Be sure to check out my other books:

Sweet Peppermint Kisses

A Portuguese Christmas

1-800-CHRISTMAS

Candleglow and Mistletoe

Aloha To Love

A Snowy White Christmas

A Christmas To Cherish (Inspirational)

and the book bundles:

Holiday Hearts Volume One

Holiday Hearts Volume Two

RECIPE FOR TINA'S CHINESE CHRISTMAS COOKIES

Ingredients
- 1 cup semisweet chocolate chips
- 1 cup Butterscotch chips
- 1 cup chow mein noodles
- 1 cup dry-roasted peanuts

Preparation Steps
1. Melt chocolate and butterscotch chips until smooth.
2. Put chow mein noodles and peanuts in a large bowl.
3. Pour chocolate mixture over the noodles and peanuts and stir until well coated.
4. Drop rounded tablespoonfuls of mixture onto wax paper. Refrigerate until set.

RECIPE FOR NANCY'S CARAMELS

6 cups sugar

   3 cups light corn syrup

   6 cups cream

   1 cup butter

   1 ½ Tsp. Salt

   1 Tbsp vanilla

Combine sugar, syrup and 3 cups cream in a large heavy saucepan. Cook over medium heat: boil about 10 minutes. Add remaining cream slowly, keeping at a boil, stirring constantly. Boil 5 minutes longer.

Add butter, 1 teaspoon at a time; stir in.

Lower heat so mixture remains at a slow boil and cook to a firm ball stage (248 degrees) (45 minutes to an hour).

Remove from heat; add salt and vanilla. Let stand 10 minutes, then pour into greased (about 12" x 17" pan). Let sit for several hours to cool before cutting and wrapping in waxed paper.

You can make 1/3 of this recipe and pour into 2 greased bread pans.

ACKNOWLEDGMENTS

An appreciative thank you to my patient husband, Dave, and our three wonderful children.

ABOUT THE AUTHOR

Josie Riviera is a USA TODAY bestselling author of contemporary, inspirational, and historical sweet romances that read like Hallmark movies. She lives in the Charlotte, NC, area with her wonderfully supportive husband. They share their home with an adorable shih tzu, who constantly needs grooming, and live in an old house forever needing renovations.

Become a member of my Read and Review VIP Facebook group for exclusive giveaways and free ARCs.

To connect with Josie, visit her webpage and subscribe to her newsletter. As a thank-you, she'll send you a free romance novella directly to your inbox.

josieriviera.com/
josieriviera@aol.com

ALSO BY JOSIE RIVIERA

Seeking Patience

Seeking Catherine (always Free!)

Seeking Fortune

Seeking Charity

Oh Danny Boy

I Love You More

A Snowy White Christmas

A Portuguese Christmas

Holiday Hearts Book Bundle Volume One

Holiday Hearts Book Bundle Volume Two

Candleglow and Mistletoe

Maeve (Perfect Match)

The Seeking Series

A Christmas To Cherish

A Love Song To Cherish

A Valentine To Cherish

Valentine Hearts Boxed Set

Romance Stories To Cherish

Aloha to Love

Sweet Peppermint Kisses

1-800-CUPID

1-800-CHRISTMAS

1-800-IRELAND

Irish Hearts Sweet Romance Bundle

The 1-800-Series Sweet Contemporary Romance Bundle

All books are available in ebook, audiobook, paperback, and Large Print paperback.

A CHRISTMAS TO CHERISH (A CHRISTIAN CONTEMPORARY HOLIDAY ROMANCE) PREVIEW

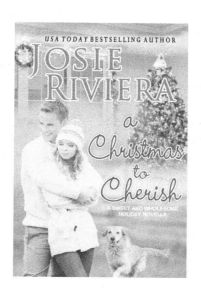

CHAPTER ONE

Emmanuelle Sumter surveyed the picturesque town of Cherish, South Carolina, brightly lit in crimson and green holiday decor. The town looked as if it had emerged from a

Christmas card. Glittering frost framed bare tree branches, and local artists were setting up their canvases for an art walk. The coldness in the air was soundless and serene, comforting in its own way.

She exited the Cherish Central train station, zippered her cobalt-blue puffer coat to her chin, and stepped onto the curb.

Who believed an actual, breathing town could resemble a holiday snow globe?

Evidently, her friend Dorothy did, considering her enthusiasm whenever she described her idyllic South Carolina town.

Emmanuelle stood on the curb and shoved her hands in her pockets. A cold December gust slapped her cheeks, sharp streams of frigid air. She swept a wisp of hair from her cheek and searched for Nicholas, Dorothy's older brother. He was supposed to pick her up. People were shouting greetings, kissing, cooing over babies. A teeming mass of humanity.

But no Nicholas.

A taxi's horn spiked. Emmanuelle jumped, an involuntary nervous reaction.

Take a deep breath. Relax. Dorothy had assured her Cherish was a safe haven, a harbor in a storm.

Repeating her mantra, Emmanuelle hailed the black-bearded taxi driver parked at the curb. She still didn't see any sign of Nicholas, so she'd take the cab.

She handed the driver her suitcase, then slid into the backseat and gave the address of Dorothy's music store, Musically Yours.

They passed charming shops decorated in glittering lights, and a sign advertising a historic home tour. A few minutes later, the driver pointed at the Musically Yours lighted outdoor sign and idled at the corner of Myrtle and Magnolia Streets.

"The store's two hoots and a holler away, ma'am." He hoisted her suitcase from the trunk and set it on the sidewalk. "We've reached your destination."

Destination. Was this where her journey ended after a year filled with pain and abuse? Did hope and encouragement wait for her in this little town?

A new life. With perseverance, she could start fresh.

"Thanks." She climbed from the taxi, paid the driver and grabbed her suitcase.

Daylight faded as dusk crept in, and she tipped her head to take in Evergreen Street. Family-owned businesses had switched on their storefront lights, transforming the town into a fairy-tale sparkle of miniature white lights. The tantalizing scent of honey roasted almonds wafted through the air. Boughs of fragrant holly tied with red velvet bows hung cheerily from tall solitary lampposts. Bright-faced children skipped by, lifting their faces skyward to catch a sprinkling of snow. Their conscientious parents followed close behind.

"Emmanuelle! You arrived right on time!" Dorothy flung open the door of the music store and pressed a welcoming kiss to Emmanuelle's cheek. Dorothy's brown hair was swept up in a French braid, her creamy complexion glowing with an enthusiasm Emmanuelle didn't recall from their days working as struggling musicians in New York.

Dorothy had lived there before moving back to Cherish, her hometown, and marrying her high school crush, Ryan Edwards. He had been an opera star in the making and had given up his touring career to settle in Cherish. They were newlyweds. They were in love.

Love. The beginning was always so alluring. It was the end Emmanuelle feared.

Dorothy regarded the departing taxi. "Apparently Nicholas didn't pick you up?"

"I didn't see him so I took a cab."

Emmanuelle turned from Dorothy and admired Musically Yours' frosty window display, bedecked in an infinite array of treble clef signs. A pine wreath, embellished in antique ornaments—tiny pianos, violins, and harps—adorned the front door.

"It's wonderful," she said. "You've worked so hard to set this up."

"Thanks. Ryan and I are still learning the business, and we're inspired by anything musical."

Emmanuelle smiled, but then shivered. "It's colder here than I expected. At least the blizzard that threatened to shut down New York never came."

"The storm hit after you left," Dorothy replied. "You escaped the worst of it."

Did she? She couldn't answer at first, finally whispering, "Hopefully."

Dorothy raised a delicate eyebrow, but Emmanuelle didn't elaborate. Sure, she'd escaped the snowstorm. An escape from George, her ex, was yet to be determined.

Please God, be with me now in my dark season, when I'm so out of place. The world around me is glowing with the promise of Christmas and I feel dark and empty inside.

She leaned forward to admire two animated polar bears sitting amidst the treble clef signs in the shop's window. Beneath a starry sky, the bears tapped drums to the tune of "Jingle Bells."

"Very clever." She couldn't help a grin. "Thanks for the invite to Cherish."

"We're thrilled you agreed to join us for Christmas." Dorothy grabbed her hands for a reassuring squeeze. She was so pleasant and gracious, Emmanuelle thought. So jovial.

On the other hand, Emmanuelle felt the opposite. All she had become in twenty-five years—a dependable, straightforward woman as well as an esteemed harpist—she'd lost in six months to George.

She'd once been like Dorothy, resilient, independent and a woman of God.

Her ex had taken it all away.

Deep in her coat pocket, her fingers worried an angel ornament she'd purchased at the New York airport. For her, the ornament symbolized the sacred Christmas season, its optimism, dreams, and promise.

She hadn't taken it out of her pocket yet.

"You've been difficult to reach these past few months." Dorothy studiously appraised Emmanuelle. "You hardly ever answered your phone."

"I've been busy with concert engagements." Emmanuelle forced her features to remain blank. "You know, musician stuff." It was a lie, and with the lie came heaviness, a wide band of disapproval. Where had her sense of decency gone?

She tightened her paisley scarf around her neck. Although the violent purple and yellow bruises had faded, she still felt self-conscious.

Dorothy guided her into the music store. "My brother will blame his forgetfulness on his new job, or that gigantic puppy he bought at the animal shelter. You'd think he'd know better at thirty years old."

"He's a good guy," Emmanuelle said. "Nicholas and I Skyped every night for months when you were in rehab."

"Thanks to you both, I'm better." Dorothy smiled. "And most important, thanks to God."

Once, Emmanuelle would have readily agreed. God was her salvation, her refuge. Now she didn't know how to answer because her faith had wavered.

Truly I tell you, if you have faith as small as a mustard seed, you can say to this mountain, "Move from here to there," and it will move. The verse from Matthew 17-20 came to her mind, a reminder of her strength. All she had to do was reach for it, if she was brave enough.

Inside the store, Dorothy ran a finger along one of the shelves, grinning when she was assured it was dust free. "Ryan and I purchased a cottage-style bungalow four blocks from here and there's an extra bedroom."

"This is your first Christmas as a married couple." Emmanuelle set her suitcase out of the way of a passing customer. "Please celebrate the holiday without me in the middle."

"I insist you stay with us."

"For an entire month?" Emmanuelle shook her head. "Insist all you want. I booked a room at the Cherish Hills Inn. You raved about the inn's accommodations being top-quality when you returned to Cherish for your brother's wedding last year."

"The wedding that didn't happen." Ruefully, Dorothy sighed. "Nicholas is still healing from the embarrassment and heartbreak."

The ending stages of love. Dreams shattered.

Without warning, the front door burst open. Instinctively, Emmanuelle held up a hand, shielding herself from view.

A heavy-set woman, her hair helmeted in a tight gray bun, ambled inside. She called out a jovial hello to Dorothy.

"Be with you in a minute, Mrs. McManus." Dorothy gave a flap of her hands, and then turned back to Emmanuelle. "Sorry. What were we discussing?"

Emmanuelle blew out a breath. This uneasiness, this fear of being followed, had to stop.

Still shaken, she kept her focus on a Mozart statue topped with a red plush Santa hat sitting on the counter.

"We were discussing the wedding that didn't happen," she replied. "Whenever Nicholas and I talked when you were in rehab, he always reminded me we should place our trust in God."

"Sadly, people change, beliefs change." Worry replaced Dorothy's earlier smile. "Hard knocks can shake the faith of the most devout. I pray he'll go to church again because he's faltered since the breakup."

Suggesting Emmanuelle put her suitcase behind the front counter, Dorothy led her past a display table. As Dorothy paused to rearrange two pairs of oboe earrings so they lined up side by side, she said, "God had other plans for him and for me. I believe things work out for the best."

Emmanuelle frowned and nodded, aborting both actions.

For Dorothy, perhaps. For Ryan. For anyone in this idyllic snow globe town. But not for me. And apparently not for Nicholas.

Her cell phone buzzed. She retrieved it from her tote bag and scanned the screen. *Unknown caller.* Her heart stopped. A telemarketer? A wrong number?

"Who is it?"

Looking up, she saw Dorothy was studying her with keen interest.

"No one." Fumbling, Emmanuelle tucked the phone back into her faux leather tote. "You're right. People change for many reasons." And she'd changed most of all. She'd been a competent, successful woman. Now a chill crept up her spine when a door opened into a harmless music store.

"Are you okay?" Dorothy asked.

"I'm fine, just tired from traveling." Emmanuelle's eyes welled with tears, and she averted her gaze. She'd applied makeup, the first time in months, attempting to conceal her sleep deprivation. The endless worrying and crying had taken a toll.

"We're organizing a concert in the town square the weekend before Christmas," Dorothy was saying. "I meant to ask you to bring your harp—"

"My harp weighs nearly eighty pounds." She picked up a pair of piano earrings and fingered the tiny keyboard. "It's in New York."

Broken. She wouldn't reveal how George had destroyed her harp in one of his lightning-fast rages. The memory caused a block of ice to form in her stomach, a block that she knew would be slow to thaw. She hated the thought of her beloved instrument, splintered into pieces, lying on a New York curb under a pile of snow.

Better the harp than you splintered into pieces.

But his shouted insults and rough slaps had been her fault. She'd provoked him.

No, no, no. Her inner voice took on a sharp edge. That was the old Emmanuelle talking. The new Emmanuelle knew she wasn't a dishtowel to be thrown around on a whim. In hindsight, she should have known George was abusive. The warning signs were there.

She blew out a breath. She'd resolved to find peace and comfort in this holiday … in this town … somewhere … and find her footing again.

*** End of Excerpt *A Christmas To Cherish* by Josie Riviera ***

Want more contemporary inspirational romances? Continue reading:

A Christmas To Cherish
A Valentine To Cherish
and my 3 book bundle:
Romance Stories To Cherish

All FREE on Kindle Unlimited!

CPSIA information can be obtained
at www.ICGtesting.com
Printed in the USA
LVHW040134151019
634128LV00008B/2827/P

9 781732 989498